Because I Didn't Know

Just Because, #3

Drew Duncan

Chapter One
Matt

I HIT end call and sighed in frustration. It had been my editor. Apparently, she had decided on a long list of 'subtle improvements' that would need to be made to my next novel. Ruth's version of 'subtle' really meant extensive reworking.

'Depth of characters, relatability of the storyline, hotness of the sex scenes,' — the list was exhausting — and to top it all off, the publisher was moving the release date forward. Three whole months forward. Panic was already setting in, and I wasn't sure I was going to make it. A point I'd argued with Ruth, but she reminded me of the nice big advance I'd been given, and that I'd better find a way to make it work.

Ever since my last three books had hit number one in the bestseller lists, Oakley Publishing had been piling on the pressure to produce more and more. Every time, they shaved time off the deadline, but they had never taken months off it before. Now this deadline was looming dangerously close on the horizon, and I wasn't sure I would make it.

Panic rising, I did the only thing I could think of and called my best friend, Toni. She always had the answers.

Toni and I had been best friends since the age of eleven. We and our other friend, Emily, had been BFFs since we met on our first day of secondary school.

"Are they having a fucking laugh?" She was always so ladylike in her conversations. "Do they think you just shit books out of your ass?"

I smiled; Toni had been like this since we met. I think that's why we became such fast friends. She was blunt, unapologetically so, and she was always right.

"You'd think so, wouldn't you? I don't know how the hell I'm meant to do it!" I sighed. "Seriously, Toni. What the hell am I going to do?"

In the silence that followed, I could just imagine the look on Toni's face as she tried to come up with a solution for me. I smirked. Her 'thinking face', she called it. I loved her, but sometimes, she was a very stereotypical blonde.

"Talk to Emily!" she finally exclaimed.

"What? Why? What good would that do?" Was this the time when the mighty Antonia didn't have a plan? Was she finally out of ideas and going to let me down after all these years?

"She's got that holiday rental company, remember? Secluded, great views of the mountains, blah, blah, blah!" I could practically hear Toni's eyes rolling.

"Toni, you know what, you might actually be a friggin' genius!"

She snorted. "Did you even doubt me, you bitch? It's the obvious choice. She's been offering it to you for ages now. Maybe it's time you took her up on it."

I considered my options for a moment. Emily had always pimped her holiday homes as secluded hideaways.

Of course, she meant it for dirty weekends and romantic getaways, but I was sure it would work out in this situation as well.

"You're right. I think I'll give her a ring and see what she can come up with. Thanks, best bitch." I laughed.

Toni chuckled too. "I am the best. I know!"

"Conceited troll."

She laughed and kissed at me down the phone. "Mwah! Love you too. Later, asshole." She hung up.

I chuckled, scrolled through my contacts, and gave Emily a call.

"Of course I have something for you, babe; you know that. As long as you don't mind my brother being there, I have a farmhouse you can stay in for free while he's fannying about, making the renovations on the latest little spot I bought. It's up by Ullswater in the Lake District. Very isolated. Perfect for you to get your work done."

My brow furrowed. "Your big brother Dean, you mean?"

"Yeah. I have him working for me as my maintenance man. He's up in the Lakes at the minute at that property. I know he's just finished redecorating the farmhouse, and now he's working on the farm itself and doing a load of stuff around the grounds. I'm planning to get some yurts in for glamping. It's off-season, so it's the perfect time to get the work done. Between you and me, you'd be doing me a favour. If you're there, he'll not be spending too much time pissing about. He'll have to actually work for fear of you reporting back to me."

"Uh, sure. I guess I can live with that, I think."

I thought about how annoying Emily's brother had been in school. I mean, to Toni he was okay, but I think that had something to do with the fact that he fancied her. I remember one time when she fell off Dean's skateboard, aged twelve. He carried her back to their house in a piggy-back while blood poured out of her knee. He had held her hand and dried her tears too as their mum picked the gravel out of her wounds. To Emily and me, he was the bane of our lives, always picking on us.

He thought he was the funniest bastard around, and was there in the background, forever doing the proverbial pigtail pulling and name-calling. Of course, in my case, he really did call me names. He called me 'Girl Toy'. I'm gay, and my two best mates are girls. He thought he was just hilarious. He had also been the first boy I had been even remotely interested in. He was good-looking, and funny, very sweet to Toni, even if he acted like he was a giant penis most of the time. He had been the first boy I wanted to look at me and think I was amazing. Instead, he called me names and made sure he was anything but interested in someone like me.

I remembered a particular time of him being nice enough to collect Toni, Emily, and me from a nightclub at the age of eighteen, only for Toni to throw up in the back of his Ford Fiesta. He'd never offered to collect her again after that night, funnily enough. I had to be honest; I think I'd fancied him for quite a few of my teenage years. Obviously, the feelings were very much unrequited.

I remembered photos Emily had shared on social media. Dean had a son and a baby momma. Yeah, this man was never going to like me the way I had liked him.

"You could get the train up, or fly to Newcastle and hire

a car or something?" Emily suggested, bringing me back to reality.

"Yeah, I'll probably just drive it. I'll have to Google it. I'll text you later with the time I'll get there. I'll sort it out now."

"Not a problem. You sort it, and I'll text you the details and text Dean so he knows when to expect you."

"You're a gem, Em. I really can't thank you enough for this."

I heard the smile in her voice. "You're welcome. Get that book done. I'm looking forward to reading it."

I groaned, said my goodbyes, and got on my laptop to look for the best route and how long it would take.

***

The next morning, I unloaded the last of my bags into the car.

"You'd better call when you get there!" Toni reminded me from the kerb.

I grinned and shook my head. "You know there's probably no coverage there, right?"

"You know we had telephones with these things called wires long before mobiles were invented, right?" my cheeky friend replied. "Emily said the farmhouse has a phone for emergencies."

"I know, I know!" I said, holding my hands up in defeat. "Just don't give the number out to anyone, okay? I'm going up there to make my deadline, distraction-free!"

Toni nodded and held out her arms for a hug. "You take care."

"I will. It's only for a few weeks. We'll head out the

second I'm back. I will be missing cocktails with my girls, and city life!" I smiled.

"Later, bitch." Toni pouted, and I waved, started the car, and headed out on the open roads for my six-hour trip.

About fifteen minutes after pulling off the motorway, I found myself within view of Ullswater, and Arthur's Pike sitting on the other side of the lake.

In the middle of all that picture-perfect scenery, I pulled off the main road onto a small single-track private road that led to a farm. There was an old stone farmhouse that had been whitewashed. It looked like something out of a romance novel. It had a heavy wooden front door, and pretty sash windows divided into twelve smaller panes of glass. Everything about the farmhouse was idyllic, and Emily had been right; it was deserted as hell. Aside from a tiny village a little way down the road, and the occasional empty holiday cottage dotted around, there was nothing.

I got out of the car and headed for the door. Just as I got to it, it sprang open, and there, filling the doorway, stood Dean. It had been years since I had last seen him. Being out of school, we didn't move in the same circles anymore. I'd had no contact with him aside from the occasional family photo he was tagged in on Emily's Facebook, which I had to admit, after Emily sharing images of him and his new son, I hadn't really been paying attention to. Okay, now I was looking, and I had to admit, I was impressed with what I saw. He was more handsome than I remembered. He was more muscular, and he had a scruffy beard on his face. I was enjoying looking at him a little more than I should have, and then he opened his mouth and ruined everything. "Well, hello, Girl Toy. Long time, no see." He smirked.

I sighed. "Dean the Dickhead. I see you've not grown up any in the years since I last saw you."

"Sorry, mate. Old habits," he said by way of an apology, extending out his hand to me. "Long time no see, huh?" He grinned a shit-eating grin. Ugh. I wanted to punch him in his sexy mouth. In that instant, he was forgiven. I couldn't resist him, and part of me wondered if he knew it.

I elbowed him in the ribs as I made my way past him.

"You know, Emily said you were working up here, and that I'd get some peace to get my work done." I huffed.

What had I been thinking agreeing to this? I *had* figured maturity would have settled in by now, and that my hormones were a thing of the past. Unfortunately, I couldn't have been more wrong.

He just looked me up and down and said nothing as I looked around the kitchen area that was beyond the front door.

There was something to the way he looked at me too. He was drinking me in, almost like he was admiring me, and I wasn't sure I liked that. I didn't need to be eye-fucked by a man who wasn't into men and definitely wasn't into me.

"What?" I snapped.

He held out his hand in front of me. "Car keys? I'm assuming you want a hand getting shit out of the car?"

Without thinking, I handed them over, and he headed to the boot of my car and started pulling my stuff out. I sighed, happy that, for now, he was occupied and away from me. I needed a cup of coffee to wake me up after travelling, and to heat me up a little too. Damn, November in the Lake District was cold. Just as I was filling my cup with hot water, Dean banged his way through the door with my bags and took them down the hallway. I opened the fridge and found a little fresh milk at the bottom of a carton; just enough to make my coffee a hint below black.

"I take mine milky with two sugars." His voice behind me made me bristle.

I glared at him and held up my mug. "Sorry. Used the last of the milk." I smirked and brushed past him again, needing to find the lounge and a fireplace. I prayed Emily would have told him to have a fire going for when I arrived.

Chapter Two
Matt

I stood warming myself by the fire as the sound of laughter and, "No, Daddy!" came down the hallway, as did a small person. They stopped in their tracks when they saw me. Dean was following the boy, grinning and with his hands up like he was chasing the child with claw hands.

I couldn't help but stare at them, a small pang of jealousy piercing through me. Dean's son was here, and the child looked a lot like his father. I'd often thought about having children, and there was the object of my teenage desire standing there with his son. Life was just not fair sometimes.

"Sorry." He smiled genuinely, ruffling the little boy's hair as he did. "Finn and I were just messing about, weren't we, buddy?"

I stared a little too long.

"Didn't Emily tell you that Finlay was going to be here with me?" I shook my head. "It's half term. He's only here until tomorrow, when his mum will collect him. He's back to school on Monday, aren't you?"

The child nodded, and still, I stared. I shook my head to

snap myself out of what probably appeared as rudeness. "Sorry." I cleared my throat and moved towards them both with an outstretched hand. "Hello, Finlay." I smiled. "I'm Matt. It's lovely to meet you."

"Finn and I were just heading to the supermarket. We needed to get some things. The cupboards and fridge are pretty bare."

I suddenly felt a pang of guilt at using the last of the milk. "Let me?" I offered sheepishly. "If you let me know where my bedroom is, I can unpack while you make a list of everything you'd like, and I can make myself useful."

Dean's forehead creased. "Aren't you here to work?"

I nodded. "I am, but every good author needs a supply of snacks before they start, and I can get those at the same time."

"Okay. If you're sure." Dean turned and pointed towards the stairs. "Head on up to the top, and it's the second door on the left."

I nodded.

"Come on, bud. Let's go and make a shopping list for Matt."

I made my way past them and followed Dean's directions. The bedroom was quite like the rest of the farmhouse. Quaint and cosy. There was a wooden floor with a large floral rug and an open brick fireplace with a log fire roaring in it. My bedroom had a beautiful wrought iron bedstead, and the most amazing handmade quilt draped over the top of a thick duvet.

Bloody hell. Is that how cold it gets at night?

I set my case on the bed and started to unpack my stuff into the beautiful pine wardrobe and dresser. Once everything was in its place, and I had my case tucked under the bed, I headed back to the kitchen to see if they had my shopping list ready for me yet.

The nearest major supermarket was about twenty minutes away in Penrith. Not exactly a quick trip to the corner shop, but I did want to make sure it was a good week or more before I had to head back out again to make another supermarket dash. I grabbed my keys, made sure my wallet was in my pocket, and went back out to my BMW 1 series.

An hour and a full boot of groceries later, just as the sky was turning the most amazing shades of pinks, purples, and oranges that I'd ever seen, I pulled into a little place called Ullswater Marina. I got out of the car and pulled my coat tight around me and my hat down over my ears as I stood on the stony shore and watched the last of the day's light disappearing behind Arthur's Pike. My mind raced to ideas of just how many people had also stood on this very beach and watched a similar sky, from tourists to ancient knights, and I felt goosebumps spread over my skin. This place would make an excellent setting for another book. I just needed to get through the one I had to finish on time first. I headed back to the car before it got too dark to see my way back to it, started it up, and got back on the winding road leading to the farm. When I parked up in the almost complete darkness, Dean knocked on the car window, scaring the life out of me again.

"Are you going to do that the entire time I'm here?" I complained as he smirked at me.

"Do what?" He grinned.

"Sneak up on me and scare the shit out of me!" I

slapped him, shoved him out of my way, and headed to the back of the car.

"Would you like some help?"

"Yes, I bloody would."

He chuckled to himself and grabbed half of the bags from the boot in one go, then carried them into the farmhouse. *Show off.* I grabbed two bags and found him in the kitchen, digging through the bags. He had my rosé in one hand and my big box of Lindor in the other.

"Is this your idea of author supplies, then?" He waved them at me and laughed.

"Oh, bugger off, Dean. Yes. Yes, it is. There's more in the boot still. Why don't you go and get it while I put all this stuff away?" I snatched my wine and chocolates back from him and shoved both into the fridge.

"I will, and then I'll get cooking. Thanks for grabbing my shopping list for me. You're welcome to join us as a thank you," he said as he walked out the door.

"What's on the menu?" I called after him.

"Curry," came the reply that echoed in the darkness.

Chapter Three
Matt

I sat at the table while Dean was cooking. "Something smells incredible."

He smirked at my compliment. "Won't be long until it's ready. Do you fancy setting the table?" he asked, waving a spatula in my direction.

"I can do that."

Without another word, we started moving around in the kitchen in unison. I was grabbing plates, knives, forks, and glasses. Dean was moving between the stove and the countertop and fridge.

I couldn't help but notice how fluidly he and I moved around the space together. We seemed to be in perfect synchronisation, never getting in the other's way, anticipating where to move next to avoid a collision. Dean poured out some wine for me and grabbed himself a beer. We lifted our plates of food and headed to the table. Dean called Finn into the kitchen.

We sat, eating our food, enjoying general chit-chat. Finn told me stories about school and what he and his friends got up to. The kid was adorable. He looked a lot like a younger version of his father, and again, I had that pang of sadness over what would never be.

When the food was done, I offered to clean up and do the dishes, while Finn and Dean disappeared off to sort a shower and PJs and everything else little kids need.

A few hours later, Finn was asleep, and Dean and I were in the living room in front of the massive fire.

"So, you're a family man now, huh?"

Dean nodded. "Yeah. e's pretty damn cool, I think. He's seven now. He wasn't what I had been expecting when I was young and dumb and fooling around with his mum."

Was that regret in his voice? Before I could think it through properly, the words were already out of my mouth. "You didn't want to have a child?"

Dean shook his head, with a quickly uttered. "No, no, no. You have it all wrong. I love Finlay and his mum, and I wouldn't be without that kid for anything in the world. It just didn't happen how or when I thought it would."

"Ah, I see."

"What about you? Had any kids, got hitched, or anything like that since I last saw you?"

I shook my head. "No, no kids. No Mr Right either, to be honest. Never found someone all that appealing after my teen years, and these days I'm too busy working to even think about it."

I lied. There had been someone. He had even proposed, but I just couldn't bring myself to do it. It wasn't that I was pining for Dean or any childhood fantasy of romance. He just didn't fit. There wasn't anything in particular that made him not for me. He wanted the white picket fence, and the little house husband and all that went with it, and that just wasn't me. I wasn't a Stepford husband by any stretch of the imagination.

"You should get around to it someday." He smiled. "I can highly recommend parenthood. I mean, sure, it can be hard work, but that kid is worth more than the universe to me."

I smiled warmly at how fondly Dean talked about his son.

We chatted more and very indirectly about our lives, skirting over the parts that neither of us really wanted to share or admit to.

As the evening progressed, we got a bit cheekier with each other, a little alcohol loosening our lips.

"You know, I'm sure you'll make a lovely house husband one day." Dean laughed when I talked about wanting to marry someday.

"You are such a misogynistic wanker."

"Ah, now, just because you're some kind of writer, doesn't mean you need to throw big words at me."

"Why? Because you can't understand them?"

He chuckled and shook his head. "No, because, as Oscar Wilde said, 'Don't use big words, they mean so little'."

What? Dean knows Oscar Wilde?

He laughed a little more at the expression of shock on my face. "What? You think because I'm brash and work with my hands all day that I have no brain to use?" He raised an eyebrow at me.

"You hide it very well."

He smirked, and I had to admit, his humour at the situation was a little infectious. I felt the corners of my mouth rise a little. "Thanks. I do try."

I snorted, and both of us said nothing more. Instead, we sat in front of the fire and enjoyed the heat in silence.

I hadn't written a word, and I was starting to feel guilty about the time I had lost so far. I headed to my room to grab my MacBook and settle back down in front of the fire. I opened my manuscript and stared at the screen. *I'm never going to do this on time.* Panic filled me, and I wondered what would happen if I didn't meet my deadline. I wondered if they would demand back my advance from the book. I was lost in my thoughts and didn't hear Dean come back into the room. A full glass of wine being set on the coffee table in front of me lifted me from my pondering.

"Thank you."

"This the book then?" He nodded at my laptop.

I closed it, set it on the table, and lifted my wine glass instead. "Yeah."

"You'll not do much with it if it's sitting on a shut laptop." He sat down in the same chair and sipped on a fresh bottle of beer.

"Probably not," I agreed, "but if I have no idea what I'm doing with it at the minute, staring at the screen endlessly isn't really going to help much either." I sighed.

Dean nodded. "Want to watch a film instead, then?" He grabbed the remote control from the coffee table.

I shrugged. "I guess it wouldn't hurt."

Forty minutes later, my laptop was forgotten, and I was enjoying *American Pie* with Dean.

"God. Stiffler makes me cringe every time." I laughed.

"Oh, 'Get some balls', Matt." He laughed.

I wrinkled my nose. "See, that's what I'm talking about. He's a douche. I don't know how they put up with him as long as they did."

Dean took a drink of his beer. "Because he's the Stiffmeister, baby! Yeah!"

I laughed and shook my head. "No."

Dean smirked and shrugged.

Silence crept over us again. We sat there enjoying the film together, but not really talking or connecting, just awkwardly present for the same experience at the same time.

When the film was over, I got up. "I think I'll head to bed. It's been a long day with a lot of travelling, and I do have a lot of work to get stuck into tomorrow. Thank you for dinner." I smiled politely.

Dean nodded.

I headed out the door, and just as I was about to start down the hallway, Dean spoke.

"Sweet dreams, Matt."

I paused and glanced back at him. "Thanks, Dean. You too."

Chapter Four
Dean

WELL, shit. That was fucking awkward. Hearing Matt Elwes was heading up here had set me on edge. Back when we were at school, he was my kid sister's gay best friend. But I wasn't out, and while I liked him, I had never had the balls to do anything about it. I mean, he was my kid sister's best friend, and that would have just been awkward. He didn't know I was gay back then. Hell, I wasn't even willing to admit I was gay back then. Instead, I flirted endlessly with their other mate, Toni.

But now, well, he was still my kid sister's best friend, and he was still younger, but he was also an adult. A handsome, smart, feisty man, and I still had the same stupid crush on him I always had. More so, because he had most definitely improved over the years I hadn't seen him, and I didn't even think that was possible.

Can you really improve on perfection?

Years might have passed, but I settled into the same familiar pattern of shit-stirring and teasing. It was easier than being open with him, and the fear he might not like me anyway. I wouldn't have blamed him if he didn't. I had spent an eternity being a proper cock around him, and I was still doing it even now.

His comments to me during the day proved, in my mind, that I was right to keep my guard up and keep taking the piss. I had to admit I was a little stung by his comment about not being able to understand big words. Sure, I work for my sister as a maintenance guy. I was good with my hands. But what he didn't know was that I made the money that bought Emily her first property. That I was her silent partner in the business, and I liked it because it left me a lot of time for reading and hanging out with my little boy. I wasn't highbrow, but I also wasn't as thick as Matt seemed to think I was. Hell, I'd even read his books. He was good.

Our general chit chat always skirted around the facts of the situation. It was easier to let him just assume I was straight and had my kid and Finn's mum, and that was it. I don't know why, but I wasn't willing to share that information just yet. I didn't want to clarify that Finn's mum and I had long parted company because I was gay. It was easier to push all thoughts of him out of my mind and remind myself that he didn't know. Besides, I had Finn to think about. A new relationship was not really what I needed right then.

I still couldn't let him go to bed without being nice to him, though. We would be there for a while together, and being a dickhead to him all the time wouldn't exactly make us staying there together easy. He had gone shopping for all of us, and I was grateful to him for that.

It wasn't long before I was heading to bed myself. I poked the fire, put the guard around it, and headed to the stairs and my bedroom. I lay there in the darkness, thinking about the fact that he was lying just a few yards away from me. My idiot brain thought about what he might be wearing, or not wearing, and not for the first time in my life, my cock throbbed because of Matt Elwes. This was going to be a nightmare. I absently palmed my dick.

Jesus, what was I doing? One day around him and I was back to jerking off like a teenager while I fantasised about him? I hoped he was going to get that book finished and be on his merry way again soon. But I wasn't sure I believed that was what I really wanted.

I couldn't get myself settled into any kind of sleep. I spent five hours tossing and turning before I finally gave up and went for a run to try and get myself focused enough to get my work done. The air was crisp, and the sun was just coming up as I pounded my way along the road. I zoned out and pushed myself hard. I needed to feel the burn. I needed to get rid of some of the tension I had brewing inside.

It was an hour later when I finally made it back to the farm. Matt must still have been asleep because there was no sign of life in the farmhouse at all. Curtains were still shut, and not a light was on, so I went back upstairs and got in the shower. Once I was dried and dressed, I got myself some coffee and sorted the fire again to keep everyone warm before heading to the kitchen to make some breakfast for Finn. His mum would be coming to collect him later.

After breakfast, I was a reasonable distance from the house, working on the tree line at the very top of the garden. All the trees needed their weakest-looking branches trimmed off. That was better than risking them falling in the middle of the next severe storm. I started the small chainsaw up and began to lop off the branches I needed to.

About fifteen minutes later, I heard it.

"HEY! HEY, ASSHOLE!"

I looked down the ladder and found Matt, red-faced, arms folded over his chest, hair in a messy 'just woke up' look.

I turned off the chainsaw and looked down at him. "What's up?"

"What's up? What's UP? It's twenty-past nine in the fucking morning, and here you are making a racket with a bloody chainsaw!"

"I have work to do." I smirked. He was just a little bit hot when he was so pissed off.

"And I was sleeping, you arrogant twat!"

"Don't you have work of your own to do?"

"That's not the point. I couldn't sleep last night. It's too fucking quiet around here."

I grinned at him and reached for the cord on the chainsaw. "Well, allow me to make some noise for you now, and then you might be able to sleep."

I didn't wait for his reply. I restarted the chainsaw and revved it over his next little rant. I put my hand to my ear like I couldn't hear him.

"UUUGHHH!!!! WANKER!!" He stomped off back to the house.

I chuckled to myself as I got back to work. He was a handful. I had to admit, if he had been any other man, that would have completely put me off, but because it was him, I found myself even more turned on. I shook my head at my reaction to him and got on with the job I had started.

Chapter Five
Matt

THE MAN WAS INSUFFERABLE. I didn't know how the hell I was going to last much longer with him and not end up killing him. He was a prick. I hated him. I stomped back down the garden and into the farmhouse. It was damn cold, and the frosty dew had leaked through my slippers. My feet were soaked. I kicked them off and pulled on some fluffy socks instead, heading back to the kitchen to get myself some breakfast and tea. With the noise outside, it was highly unlikely that I would be getting any more sleep, so I figured I may as well make the most of it and got back to my writing.

The lack of city noise wasn't the only reason I hadn't been able to sleep. The thought of him lying there in a room on the other side of the wall really hadn't helped either. It was like being a teenager and thinking about him lying in his room, while I had a sleepover in Emily's room. Eventually, I had grabbed my laptop and started working instead. I reread what I had written during the night. There was a hint of sexual tension in it, and I couldn't help but wonder if that was because of how the situation here was making me feel. Horny, teenage, and frustratingly angry.

There was a noise somewhere in the house, and Finn appeared in the doorway soon after.

"What are you doing on your computer?" he asked me and appeared at my side.

"I'm writing a story for grown-ups."

"I like stories."

It was hard not to reply with warmth. "Do you, darlin'? Does Daddy read stories to you?"

"Daddy reads to me when I get into bed, but he has his own stories too."

I grinned. *Was that so?* "Do you like daddy's stories?" I asked.

Finn screwed up his face. "Ugh." He sighed. "They're boring. They don't have any pictures."

I tried not to laugh. "What if I told you what my story was about, and you could make me a picture for it?" I suggested.

Finn nodded.

"Well, it's about a handsome prince and he lives at the top of a very high tower," I explained.

"Does he kill a dragon?" Finn asked excitedly.

I hmmed. "Well, I think if you can draw me a dragon, I might just have to put it in my book this time."

"Yes!" Finn shrieked in delight.

"Let's get to work then." I grinned, and Finn pulled out a drawing book and some pencils from his backpack, which had been hanging on the back of the chair.

I lifted my laptop and began to write...

.   .   .

The man couldn't get any more fucking annoying if he tried. I had a job to do. I was there to make sure the penthouse apartment looked terrific when Billy Dylan, the CEO of the biggest hotel chain in the States, got back to what was to be his Manhattan hideaway. Yet, there Nick was, being a complete asshole.

"You're not the only damn contractor I can hire, you know?" I grumbled at him.

He just gave me that infuriating smirk of his that was sexy and frustrating all at the same damn time. "Well, darlin', you're not the only interior designer. I happen to know Billy Dylan. One word from me, and you'll be fired." His Texan drawl really didn't help matters. He was threatening to get me sacked from the best job I had landed in the six years I had been an interior designer, and all I could think about was how the sound of his voice was making my body hum. Bastard.

I decided to call his bluff. "Nick, you can tell Mr. Dylan anything you like. I'm damn good at what I do, and he'd find it very hard to replace me."

Nick leaned in, trapping me against a new wall they were putting in. "Why don't you show me what you do, and I'll let you know if I think you're any good at it." His mouth was inches from mine. His smell, manly cedarwood and musk, filled my nostrils, and the hint of something sexual in the way he spoke to me had every inch of me responding to him.

My nipples hardened, my cock throbbed, and I held my breath. I stared at him defiantly, challenging him to do more. His stare got more intense, and I watched as his eyes darkened and his pupils dilated. For a split second, he was going to make his move, until his foreman called him.

"Hey, Nick! The delivery truck is here with the drywall

and the cement for the flooring in the master bathroom. He's got those Italian marble tiles we ordered too."

"It's about time they showed up," He mumbled against me, not moving. "I'm coming now," He shouted back over to Lester, the foreman, before pushing himself off the wall and away from me.

I couldn't move. I couldn't even think straight. Something had been about to happen with Nick. And now I was just standing there, frozen, a wanton mess, turned on and frustrated as fuck.

This was going to be a long project...

Chapter Six
Dean

"Hello?" I barked down the phone.

"Who pissed in your cornflakes?" Jess asked me.

"Shit. Sorry, Jess. I'm just pissed off with the guest Emily arranged to be here while I'm working here."

I heard the snort in her voice when I said it. "I see someone is still affected by Matt's presence then."

I shook my head, even though she couldn't see me. "He chewed my fucking balls off this morning because I was working with the chainsaw!" I growled.

"What time was that?" Jess asked me.

I rolled my eyes. "About half nine."

There was a sigh, and I already knew I had been in the wrong. "I'm not surprised the poor bastard chewed your nut sack off, darlin'. I mean, who the fuck uses a chainsaw that early?"

I rubbed my head in frustration. Jess was not meant to be taking Matt's side. "Wouldn't have been an issue if he wasn't here. Anyway, aren't you meant to be coming here to collect Finn?" I asked, changing the subject, considering the conversation about Matt done.

"Oh, I am. We're visiting Grandpa this weekend and then back to school on Monday. He still drawing his comic book?"

"He is. Camped out beside Matt at the minute." I smiled.

Jess was Finn's mum. My last girlfriend before she decided I needed to come out. Jess lived three hours from here, but her dad lived in Penrith, so this location was handy enough for her compared to some of the places I worked on for Em.

"I'll see you in a few hours then, won't I!" I grinned.

I heard the affection in her voice. "I know, but I always like to check on how my boys are doing. Oh, and Dean, make some lunch for Matt. As a way of making it up to him for the noise?" Jess suggested. Ever the peacekeeper was my adorable ex-girlfriend.

"I guess." I knew she was right, but I wasn't ready to admit it. I did need to make it up to Matt about the chainsaw. I didn't realise he had been up all night too. I guess I had never really thought about the times authors work. "I'll see you when you get here, okay? Drive safe."

I said my goodbyes, hung up the phone, and thought about what Jess had suggested. It wouldn't hurt to be at least civil to Matt, right? I mean, the nicer I was, the easier hit work would be, and he could complete it, leave, and let me get back to my life as normal. Yeah. I tried to convince myself that was a plan.

Fifteen minutes later, we were sitting around the table in the farmhouse. The kitchen wasn't completely finished yet, but it was coming along nicely. I at least had cabinets and counters now. That was a vast improvement on how it had been a week ago. Of course, I'd done that because a guest was coming, and while Finn had already been staying here, it didn't hurt that the kitchen hadn't been at least some way usable.

"I think I owe you a bit of a sorry for earlier this morning," I mumbled in the corner, glancing sheepishly at him.

He looked up at me, thinking about his reply. I waited to see if I would get another ear-bashing, or if I was being let off the hook for now.

He said nothing about it. "Thank you for lunch. I get so engrossed in what I'm doing that sometimes I can forget simple things like eating and drinking."

"You're welcome." I smiled and handed him a plate of sandwiches and a bowl of soup.

"I like my soup," Finn piped up, looking to be included in the conversation.

"It's lovely, isn't it?" Matt smiled at Finn. "Thank you." He nodded at me. "And I'm sorry too, Dean. I hadn't slept well, and when I don't sleep, I get up and write instead. I'd been up for most of the night before finally passing out."

I nodded, took my own plate, and looked at him. "In that case, I'm definitely sorry I woke you this morning."

He smiled, accepting my apology. We sat in tense silence until I couldn't take it any longer. "So, how's the book going?" I asked between mouthfuls of warming soup.

"Not too bad so far. Now I've settled into it, I guess I can understand what my editor was getting at."

I nodded. "So, what's this one about?"

"You really want to know?"

He thought I was just humouring him. "I really want to know."

He thought about it. "Well, it's frenemies to lovers."

Well, that sparked my interest. "Oh, right. What, like,

people who hate each other and then end up in the sack?" I watched his face as he grimaced just a little at my question.

"What's in the sack, Daddy?"

"Uhhh..."

"Daddy's being silly. He means having a sleepover. Sack is another word for bed."

"That's weird." Finn giggled.

"It is." Matt nodded. "It's because, in the olden days, the mattress on your bed was made from a sack full of hay. Isn't that funny!"

Finn grinned, and I stared. I hadn't thought about what I was saying in front of him, yet Matt had handled it beautifully. I was in awe.

He looked at me. "Yes, that's pretty much it."

'*Thank you,*' I mouthed, and he nodded in acknowledgement.

I thought about it. I knew only too well what he was talking about in his book. The boy in the same social circle as the other boy, and they end up with awkward fuckwittery because that's a million times easier than just admitting they like each other in case it makes it too weird for everyone else. Did he really think that kind of thing could happen? Did he ever see it happening between us? Jesus, could I see it happening between us? I chuckled at my own stupidity, and he stared at me.

"So, you really think that's possible? You think people who appear to hate each other can end up *you know*?" I chuckled nervously.

His expression grew dark. "Why wouldn't it happen? Don't you think my book is realistic? Can't people hate each other and then change their minds? Or secretly like each other the whole time?"

I raised an eyebrow at him. That went from zero to off the fucking charts in a few seconds.

"That wasn't what I meant, Matt," I soothed.

"Sorry, I just... well, I haven't slept much, have I? It's making me a bit of an arsehole."

Finn gasped. "That's a rude word."

"Sorry." Matt looked sheepishly at us both.

"I'm sorry too, Matt. I didn't mean to offend you."

"You didn't, really. I'm just worried sick about it, and it's a concept I'm already fighting with my editor about. I just don't like having to justify it as a storyline to someone who thinks it's all nonsense because that's just not how it works." Awkward silence returned.

Fuck.

I hadn't meant it like that at all. In the world of Dean Law, that was exactly how things worked, because I wanted it with Matt. Years ago, I resisted him. I walked away, and I appeared like an insensitive arsehole and kept him away from me. But not anymore. I couldn't. I had to be honest with myself and admit I wanted him, and the thought that he was writing a book about the exact scenario we were in made me genuinely curious as to whether or not he really thought it could happen. He wouldn't write it if he didn't know it was possible. Right?

I shook my head. Thinking like that was the most unhelpful course of action I had contemplated to date. I needed to escape. I needed to go and do some good old-fashioned manual labour. Again.

Chapter Seven
Matt

I THANKED Dean for lunch and made my excuses about needing to get back to work. I stood in the kitchen of the farmhouse minutes later, not really sure what my next move would be. I had overreacted when he questioned the story-line of the book, but not because I thought he was picking at my writing skills. I was worried he didn't believe it was possible that two people who seemed to hate each other would be able to fall in love, or at least fall in lust. And when he questioned it, I had to admit, that stung. I didn't know why, but I wanted him to be thinking about me. I wanted him to be thinking we could make that move from almost enemies to friends. But, from his reaction, it didn't seem like something like that was at all possible.

I heard the farmhouse door slam, and I watched as he disappeared around the corner, heading to the barn. I sighed, resigned myself to the mess of the situation, and went back to the living room in front of the fire. I lifted my laptop from the coffee table and figured I would try to get some more words done before my deadline...

. . .

"*What the fuck is this?*"

I heard Nick's complaints even before I got into the room. "You wanted to see me?" I smiled with fake cheer.

"Darlin', I know you were put on this project to try me, but would you care to explain what the ever-loving fuck this is?"

I looked at the massive piece of carved granite he was pointing to. "That would be Mr. Dean's Zen Fountain," I replied matter-of-factly.

This had not been my idea in the design process, but it was a feature he had seen online, specifically asked for, and nothing would persuade him away from.

"A Zen Fountain?" Nick echoed.

"Yes."

"And where, in God's name, am I meant to put this thing?" He was waving his hands around in frustration.

I smirked; the temptation to tell him exactly where he could put the giant piece of stone was a little too much for me to bite back. "Is that really something you want an honest answer to?"

He glared, and I stood a little straighter. I was not backing down over this one. He moved into my personal space again. "Boy, I will take you over my knee and spank your ass red if you dare open your sassy little mouth and utter the words I think you're about to."

Fuck. That was one hell of a threat, and with the already noticeable heat between us, I bit my tongue, thinking about how much I wanted that to play out. I mean, I hated the man, but the notion of being bent over his lap, his hands heating my ass in the best way possible... My filthy mind was working overtime on that one.

"I didn't think so." He took my silence as surrender.

I rolled my eyes and answered anyway. "It's for the main lobby area, right where you get off the elevators. Mr. Dean thought it would make a nice focal point. Or, at least, that's what he had in mind."

I didn't like it any more than Nick did, but after that reaction, there was no way in hell I was going to say anything to him about it. I wasn't going to agree with him. Not one bit. I liked this game a lot more with us on opposite sides of the fence from one another.

"Oh, and Nick," I added as I turned to walk away. "You can look at my ass now because these red pants are the only way you'll ever see it that colour. Are we clear?"

I didn't wait for his answer, I just walked away without looking back.

I was finally in the zone; my fingers were flying over the keys like a man possessed. It was fantastic, and then it started.

BANG! BANG! BANG!

"You have got to be kidding me!" I slammed my laptop shut and set it back on the coffee table.

BANG! BANG! BANG!

I grabbed my boots and pulled them on before stropping outside to try and find the source of the noise once again.

BANG! BANG! BANG!

When I rounded the corner of the farmhouse, there Dean was, up a ladder, hammering some facia in place.

BANG! BANG! BANG!

"OI!" I roared at the bottom of the ladder in his general direction.

His shoulders flopped forward and he sighed. "Sorry, Matt. You're not the only one with work to do around here."

"On a deadline, are you?"

"As it happens, I am."

"Well, I'm on a tighter one, and I need to get this fucking book finished, and every time I'm getting somewhere, you start kicking up a racket!"

I was so angry with him he was lucky to find himself at the top of his ladder still. I was about ready to shake him down from it and sit on him to take his hammer away.

He started to come down towards me.

"What are you doing?"

He raised an eyebrow. "I'm coming down the ladder."

I glared. "Oh, aren't we witty."

He stopped and glared back. "Would you like a solution, or are you going to keep standing there and complaining like a little bitch? I can go back up and start hammering again if you like?" he said, gesturing with his hammer back towards the roof.

I folded my arms and huffed. I wasn't about to agree with him, but I wasn't about to tell him to get on with his work either. I needed to have even a little silence. I watched him as he got off the last rung and looked at me. "Follow me."

I stood still, not doing what he was suggesting. I was boring holes into the back of his head. This had to be a trick. I would move, he would lock me in the farmhouse or something, and go back to hammering, just to annoy me.

"Are you coming?" He gestured.

Ugh. "Fine!" I stropped after him as he went into the farmhouse. He made his way to the stairs and headed up. "Where are you going?"

"This is where the solution is."

I glowered at him. "Dean, I don't know what your magic solution is, but I don't think it's upstairs."

He just laughed at me. "Fine, stand there and huff. This will only take a minute."

I stood there, my anger simmering below the surface until he reappeared from his room.

"Here." He thrust an iPod and some headphones at me.

I looked at them and then looked at him. "What do I want these for? I have music on my laptop. That's really not the issue here."

He sighed. "They're noise cancelling."

"Oh." Well, didn't I feel like a dickhead. "Thank you."

He nodded. "You're welcome, and if you find the noise is still getting through, just let me know and I'll figure something else out."

I thanked him again, feeling a little ashamed of myself, and Dean headed back to the work he was doing. I went into the living room, sat back on the sofa, got my laptop back into my lap and scrolled through his iPod to see what he had on there. I found a playlist at the bottom of a long list only named with a heart emoji. I was intrigued. I scrolled to it and selected it. I was presented with a list that surprised me. It reminded me of a lot of the times I had shared, for better or for worse, with my best friend's brother.

That track when he collected us all from a nightclub for my eighteenth birthday and Toni threw up in the back of his car. The track I never stopped singing with his sister the summer we were sixteen. Almost every single song reminded me of a time when Dean had been close by.

I tried not to overthink the list. It was just a coincidence. It didn't mean anything. I put the headphones on my head, and the banging that had restarted outside disappeared. Dean had worked his magic, after all.

I reread what I had been writing and let the trip down memory lane wash over me as I hammered away on the keyboard, driving my characters forward in their lust-fuelled loathing of each other. I didn't want to think about the possibility of anything happening between Dean and me.

Chapter Eight
Dean

I WAS STILL WORKING up the ladder when Jess's car pulled in front of the farmhouse and she beeped the horn. I made my way down the ladder, over to the driver's door, and was greeted by Jess stepping out. I hugged her and kissed her on the cheek.

"Good drive?" I asked

"Mummy!" Finn shrieked with delight and bounced out through the door of the farmhouse.

"Hello, little buddy. Did you miss me?" She grinned at him, giving him a big kiss, hugging him tightly in her arms.

Matt appeared at the doorway. Jess grinned at me with a raised eyebrow and moved past me towards him.

"This is Matt, Mummy. He writes stories, and he let me draw a dragon for the story."

Jess smiled and held out her hand for Matt to shake. "Well, aren't you a lucky boy," she said, acknowledging Finn's commentary. "Nice to meet you, Matt." She was warm and welcoming to the man I had fantasied about even when we were together. In that moment, I knew she was right to be shot of me. She would always deserve so much better. I hoped the new boyfriend she had was going to be exactly that.

Jess turned and carried Finn back over to the car, and I grabbed Finn's bag from the house.

"Wait!" Finn insisted before he got into the car. He jumped down, ran over to Matt, and hugged him as he stood watching everything. "Thank you for letting me draw a dragon for you." He grinned against Matt.

Matt hugged my son back and told him he was welcome. I was feeling a little in awe of the impression Matt seemed to have made on my son. He didn't warm to people that quickly normally.

Once everyone was settled into the car again, I said my goodbyes.

"You be damn careful on that road," I warned Jess. "Text me when you get to your dad's."

She smiled. "I will, I promise. Say bye to Daddy," she prompted Finn.

"Bye, Daddy!" He waved, squirming in the backseat.

I waved as Jess set off, watching as her car disappeared out of sight.

I worked outside for the rest of the afternoon. I didn't want to suffer the wrath of Matt again. I was happy to just keep busy and get on with my work. I thought about heading in, getting a shower, and taking myself to the local pub for a change of scenery. But shortly after having that idea, I found myself wondering if 'the Rottweiler' that had taken up residence in the farmhouse for the foreseeable future would also want to have a meal out. Only one way to find out.

When he didn't hear me knock, I opened the door and

went in. He was still hard at work on his laptop in front of the fire. He was even singing along with a track he was listening to. I thought he might notice me approaching out of the corner of his eye. But I was wrong.

"Matt," I said, and touched his arm.

He let out a screech and jumped, his laptop almost falling to the floor had I not reached out to catch it.

"Sorry." I chuckled.

"Jesus Christ, Dean. You almost gave me a bloody heart attack! You've got to stop fucking doing that!" His hand was on his chest as though it would calm his breathing and heart rate.

I smiled apologetically. "I was just wondering if you would like to go out to the local pub and get some dinner? I thought you might like the change of scenery since you've been here all day working away."

He looked me up and down, evaluating me. I thought his answer was going to be no after everything today, but I was wrong. "I could definitely eat, and yes, a local pub sounds quite nice."

I grinned and nodded. "You have to be ready in twenty minutes or the deal's off."

He jumped off the sofa and headed for the bathroom. "You have a deal."

Thirty minutes later, we were walking in through the door of the pub not even half a mile farther up the coast of the lake. "Brackenrigg Inn," he read from the sign above the door.

I held the door open for him. "You'll love it. You might even have to put it in a book somewhere."

He laughed and headed inside. The bar was attached to the local hotel, and it was all wooden-beamed ceilings and old stone walls. It was quaint and something I knew he would love.

"Oh, wow. This place is awesome!" He grinned and made his way to a table. There was a fire roaring in the hearth, and the welcome was always warm.

"Alright, Dean," one of the regulars called over as we settled ourselves.

"Evening, Donald," I replied with a bob of my head.

Matt looked at me with a puzzled look. "Do you know everyone here?"

I smiled. "Some."

"Are you here regularly?"

"Emily has a few properties in the area. I like to get up here any time I can when it's off-season."

I was there so often I was starting to look at it as a home away from home if I was really honest. There was just something about the atmosphere, the locals, and the scenery around the area, and the lake itself that appealed to me.

I grabbed two menus from the bar and went back up when we had picked what we were going to have. I wasn't going to drink that evening. I was driving, and I didn't really fancy the walk back to the farm at that time of year. Matt ordered a glass of wine, and we sat and chatted a little while we waited for our food.

"I'm sorry about how I've been today," he said, looking at me. "I know I was a bit of a cock, but this book has me pulling my hair out."

I nodded. "I get it. I honestly don't know how you do it."

He looked at me like I had said something alien. "Really?" He chuckled. "You always said I was a space cadet with a very vivid imagination who talked a load of shit."

Christ.

I snorted. He wasn't wrong. I had said exactly those words to him, and on more than one occasion. I didn't have an answer to that one at all. I merely shrugged and admitted defeat. "That's true, but not many can come back from a comment like that and make a career out of it."

He laughed, shaking his head at me, and took a long sip from his glass. I sat there, staring at him, transfixed by his mouth on the glass and his tongue on his lips. I couldn't look away, and he caught me, clearing his throat nervously. Both of us were saved from further awkwardness when the food arrived at the table.

"Ack, hello, Dean, love. You back again? And who's this lovely-looking fella?" The waitress, a lovely older woman called June, smiled at us.

"Ah, June, I thought you might miss me if I stayed away too long."

June laughed and gave Matt a wink. "Jesus, would you look at that," she said to Matt. "Flirting with me, and I'm old enough to be his mother."

Matt and I laughed and made small talk with her.

Matt laughed with June and glanced over at me, his cheeks flushed with a little pinkness.

"Here you go, love. Watch now, that plate's warm," June warned, setting the plate of food down in front of my guest. Matt smiled kindly and thanked her. "If you want dessert, you just let me know."

I laughed. "I hope you have my favourite, June?"

She rolled her eyes as she walked off. "Like we would get away with not having any for you."

I snorted and stabbed some fries with my fork, shovelling them into my mouth.

"What's your favourite?" Matt asked.

I chewed a little before replying. "Sticky toffee pudding with home-made vanilla ice cream." I smiled. Matt smirked. I hoped he was remembering the same thing I was.

Matt had been to our house, and he, Toni, and Emily had all cooked a course each for a meal they made for the whole family.

Em had made the starter; I don't even remember what it was anymore. Toni had made a fantastic roast chicken dinner, and Matt had made a sticky toffee pudding with butterscotch sauce and a home-made vanilla ice cream. I'd never really liked desserts until that point. But there was just something about the fact that he prepared it that made it the most delicious thing I had ever tasted in my life. I couldn't lie; I had never had one since that came close to being as perfect-tasting as the one he made that night.

The evening progressed with more general chatter. Matt swapped his wine for fruit juice since I wasn't drinking, and we just talked about where life had taken us for the years since we had last seen each other. We had dessert; it still didn't taste as good as his, not that I would admit that.

"Can I ask about that?"

My brow creased. "About Jess?"

Matt nodded.

"I didn't realise you were still with Finn's mum. I mean, from Emily's Facebook I knew you had a child, but I don't think I've ever seen Jess in any of the photos."

I shook my head. "I'm not with anyone."

Matt frowned. "But I thought…"

"Wrong, you thought wrong," I interrupted. "Jess is my ex."

"Oh, sorry. So, you've not got a girlfriend then?"

I smirked. "No, and I'm not going to have one either."

Matt looked a little confused

I continued. "I was a kid when I got with Jess. It wasn't serious, or at least I didn't see it that way. We were fooling around, and a few months in, Jess told me she was pregnant."

"Ah, so not so serious got serious really quickly."

I nodded. "It scared the shit out of me, and it made me face up to things that, honestly, I hadn't been ready to face up to before. Things I really should have faced up to. But again, young, dumb, just trying to fit in too much instead of being myself."

"What did it make you face up to? That you had to grow up and face the responsibility of a kid on the way?"

"Well, some of it was that, and some of it was because I wasn't being true to who I really was because I'm gay." Matt's eyes widened, and I continued. "I guess I just didn't want to admit it to myself back then. The reality of having a child with someone really does put your life into perspective for you. Jess was amazing. I think she kinda knew before I was ready to admit it. And despite being pregnant and facing the prospect of us breaking up and all that, she supported me through it. I love her. I will never not love her, but romantically, she's just not it for me."

"I didn't know..." Matt seemed genuinely surprised by my revelation.

"That I'm gay?"

He made a face and nodded. "I mean, I just never saw it."

"I hid it well. I'll be honest, I used to envy you. You knew you were gay, and you made no apologies for it. You just were who you were."

He laughs, and it was a warm, rich sound I could have got used to hearing. "It wasn't that easy," he admitted. "I mean, come on. You used to call me Girl Toy."

I winced. I did, and I had been a jerk. "I'm sorry about that. I should never have called you that. It was just some silly throwaway remark because my mates thought it was funny, and I was... well, I was a cock."

He smiled when he looked at me, and I felt something inside me melt. "Yes, you were. Where the hell did that name even come from?"

I rolled my eyes when I thought about how my friends had come up with the name for me to start calling Matt by. "It was because you were like the token gay in the group. They assumed you were like a doll to Toni and Emily, a toy to play with, and they called you Girl Toy for letting yourself be what they saw as emasculated." I cringed. It was the most ridiculous nonsense, and I had helped my friends at the time perpetuate it.

Matt shook his head. "Wow, that's some serious bullshit right there. I'm starting to see why you didn't think you could be yourself in that group."

I agreed. "Best thing I did was to get rid of them. But I'm glad it all worked out how it did. I would have missed out on having Finn had I not been in their company for that period in my life. And I wouldn't swap that little boy for the world."

Matt smiled warmly. "He's a damn cute kid."

I grinned. "He is." There was a short pause, and I had to ask. "What about you? You just never found that someone?"

Just as Matt was about to answer, the barman, Jamesy, called to me.

"Hey, Dean." When I acknowledged him with a nod, he

continued. "Have you seen the weather? They're talking snow. Amber warnings all over the place."

Shit. "Amber? For when?" Jamesy gestured for me to come over to the bar and have a look at the TV tucked out of the way. "I'll be back in a second." I smiled at Matt and headed over to the bar.

The barman was right; a huge freak storm was heading in from the Atlantic, and it was bringing with it a hell of a lot of snow. They were predicting high winds and six to twelve feet drifts. They were advising people to get in as many supplies as they could and to prepare themselves that the power would go out, and not to travel unless absolutely necessary. All this was expected to hit mid-afternoon on Saturday.

I paid our bill, thanked Jamesy for the heads up, and took my seat opposite Matt again.

"What was all that about?" He laughed.

"There's a freak snowstorm heading this way. From the sounds of it, it's going to be pretty bad."

He looked at me like I was talking nonsense. "It can't be that bad, surely?"

I nodded at him. "Oh, it can get pretty bad up here." I couldn't believe he wouldn't think an amber storm warning wasn't a big thing. "Snowed in. No power, no phone. Don't forget, we're quite isolated up here. This isn't the big city, Matt."

He held his hands up in defeat. "Okay!"

I sighed. "Come on. Time to head back. I'll need to get us ready for that storm coming in tomorrow."

He shrugged and followed me as I got up to leave.

When we got back to the farm, Matt stood looking up at the night sky. "Look at that. Not a cloud to be seen, and a myriad of history spread out before us, twinkling as stars that could be long dead for all we know."

I glanced up, taking in what he had said. I could see why he picked writing. There was a specific way his mind worked and the way he phrased things that told a story people didn't usually think of.

"Come on, you, before we freeze out here." I tilted my head towards the farmhouse door and started towards it. He stood his ground, his eyes fixed on the wonder he held in front of him for a moment longer before joining me inside.

"Nightcap?" I asked, pulling a bottle of scotch from the cupboard.

He raised an eyebrow. "I wouldn't mind." He smiled.

I chuckled, grabbed two glasses, and poured us both half a tumbler each. He glanced at his glass with wide eyes when he took it from me. I had been a little generous with the measure. We headed into the living room, sitting in front of the dying embers of the fire, still warm with a soft glow.

"Thank you for dinner." He smiled, sipping from the glass in his hand.

I watched him as he did. His eyes closed as he felt the burn of the scotch in his throat, but he was apparently not new to the taste as he didn't cough or sputter as the liquid heated him from the inside.

"You're welcome," I replied, taking a bigger sip from my own glass, feeling it catch me in the throat. More silence expanded out between us. I didn't remember ever being this awkward around him when we were younger.

Matt sighed, downed the rest of his drink, and set the glass on the coffee table. "I think I'm going to go to bed." He stood, and apparently, his drink hit him as he wobbled on his feet. I quickly abandoned my drink beside his empty glass and stood, grabbing his arms to steady him.

He gripped my arms and shook his head. "Oh!" he exclaimed. "I think that went right to my head." He giggled.

Oh, it definitely has.

He tightened his grip on my biceps and looked at me, biting his lip.

"You okay?" I asked, holding his gaze.

"Uh-huh." He was staring at me, and I felt it everywhere.

He swallowed. My glance wandered to his throat, and my mind wandered to what it would feel like to taste the delicate skin right there. He cleared his throat. "I should get to bed." His mouth said the words, but his body stayed firmly in my arms as I held him up.

"Okay," I agreed, again, neither of us moving.

"Night then," he said, and leaned forward, placing a kiss on my cheek. When he pulled away from me, there was a momentary pause, and I watched his eyes trace over my lips.

Fuck, yes, Matt. Go on and take a taste.

In the blink of an eye, the moment was gone, and he steadied himself on his feet and let go of me, moving past and heading for the door. "Sweet dreams, Dean." He smiled as he headed to his bedroom.

I watched him leave, grabbed my glass, downed the rest of my drink, and stared at the doorway he had been standing in just moments before. Fuck.

I headed back to the farmhouse before I did something I would regret and found myself in his room. Besides, it was still the very thing I hadn't admitted to Matt about myself. It was still my 'secret'.

Chapter Nine
Matt

WHEN I OPENED my eyes the next morning, I lay there and stared at the ceiling, thinking about what almost happened the night before. I had nearly kissed Dean. I'd wanted to kiss him, and I think he would have been more than happy to kiss me back. Thank God I hadn't, because I honestly don't believe I would have been able to stop if I had. Years of fantasy and frustration over him would have come pouring out. I lay there, rubbing my face, trying to stop over-thinking the might-haves and the what-ifs, and focus on the things I needed to.

My book was progressing nicely. It had only been two days, but I was getting a lot of inspiration, and despite how pissed off I had been the day before, there were a lot fewer distractions there compared to what I would have had at home. I resolved to keep up that tempo, get my arse out of bed, and get back to work on the book. Nothing else mattered. Not the fictional scenarios my brain was plotting out with Dean; the kisses, the touching, and whatever else my mind wandered to. No, the book was the only thing I needed to be spending my imagination on for the next week or so.

When I passed by his bedroom door, I saw all the curtains were pulled back, his bed was made, and he was nowhere in sight in the farmhouse. When I got to the kitchen, I could see the truck wasn't in the driveway outside either.

I made myself a coffee, grabbed a shower, and took myself for a short walk down the road to the campsite not far from the farm. I stood on the shore and let the lapping of the water soothe me. The wind was picking up, and it was brisk and refreshing. I thought about the book, the characters, where I wanted them to end up, and I walked back up to the farmhouse with a clearer head and a lot of new enthusiasm for what I needed to do.

I was working away when I heard the front door slam. I glanced up and saw Dean standing in the doorway to the living room. "Hey," I called out.

"Hey yourself. How's the book?"

I shrugged. "It's progressing well. Keeping busy?"

"Well, with the storm coming in, I thought I should get prepared. We'll need candles, logs, coal. All that kind of thing. And I got a wind-up radio, just in case. I'm just heading into the attic to check the roof is still good."

"You really think it's going to be that bad?" I asked, still in disbelief that this was going to turn out as they said. I mean, how many times a year did we get weather warnings for something, only for it to pan out to be nothing much to complain about?

Dean looked at me with intent. "I know it will be that bad." He paused for dramatic effect. "I need to get back to work now. There are still logs to sort before the storm comes in."

I nodded, slid his headphones back on, and kept on typing.

The only reason I moved when I did was that my stomach had started to growl. I got up and headed outside to see if I could see Dean anywhere, and check if he had eaten yet. I didn't get too far when I overheard him on the phone to someone.

"Yeah, I know. I'll be careful, okay... Yeah, I love you too. I'll see you soon."

It stopped me in my tracks. Did Dean really just tell someone he loved them? Hadn't he said he wasn't with anyone just last night? Maybe I had been kidding myself that I'd been getting all these signals from him. Maybe I had only been seeing what I wanted to see. My stupid schoolboy crush turned from fantasy to reality. Now the reality of it seemed to be slapping me in the face and showing me how wrong I had it.

Dean heard me and turned. He clearly read my expression in no time at all and smirked. "That was Emily. Just checking if we're going to be okay in the farmhouse with the storm coming."

"Ahh."

Well, didn't I feel like a prize arsehole for assuming the worst. I blamed it on being around Dean. He was seriously under my skin.

Chapter Ten
Dean

I HAD to laugh at Matt's reaction to the snow, but I understood it mostly. He was a city boy, and this kind of thing almost never happened in the city. Warnings got issued, and things never appeared, but in the north, that threat was genuine.

I had checked the latest on my tablet earlier; the reports were bad. If things got as bad as they were expecting, phones and power would go down, roads would close, and we really would be completely cut off.

Jess had called. She and Finn were enjoying time with her dad. Finn had been telling him all about his dad's new friend who was putting his dragon picture in his book, and how amazing that was. I couldn't help but smile that he seemed to have taken a shine to Matt.

I had also given some serious thought to whether or not I wanted to tell Matt it would be more sensible to head back to a hotel in Penrith or something for the duration of the storm. But then I thought about being stuck out there in the middle of nowhere with him, with nothing else to occupy us, and I couldn't resist waiting to figure out how that would go. I was a selfish bastard. I knew we wouldn't be at any real risk of life. The farmhouse was well looked after. We had enough supplies of food, and in the fuel for the fire. I had no doubts that while we would be suffering a little with the lack of heat and power, we were perfectly safe.

I wanted to know what would happen between us. I could see it happening one of two ways; either we killed each other, or whatever the hell was going on between us would finally come to fruition.

When I made my decision to stay and not say anything about leaving, I went out to make sure we had the kinds of things we might need. I got matches, candles, and a lot of dishwasher salt to use to clear some snow. I bought some extra food, some milk, anything I could think of that we might need. I even managed to pick up a wind-up radio. That way, we would at least be able to have something other than silence.

The wind was really picking up when I started to split logs and stack them by the back door. I filled the buckets that lived by the fire; one with coal and one with logs. I made sure everything was ready.

By the time I was just about satisfied with the size of the log pile I had, the snow had started. Big, thick flakes floating around in the wind hid almost everything from sight beyond the end of the garden. Within twenty minutes, everything was covered with at least an inch of white. I stood watching the snow fall by the back door when it opened, and Matt appeared beside me. "Wow, it's really coming down, isn't it?"

I smiled. "It is. It's pretty now, but it'll be a pain in the ass by tonight."

He laughed and touched my arm as he did. It was a

friendly, innocent gesture, but I felt my skin burning from his touch, even through my coat and jumper.

"Do you think we'll be okay out here? I mean if it gets as bad as everyone seems to think it will?"

I turned to look at him, placed my hands on his shoulders, and looked at him carefully. "You are completely safe here. I wouldn't be staying out here myself if it wasn't safe. I have Finn to think about after all."

I held his gaze. I wanted to say more. I wanted to let him know just how much he would always be safe with me, but it seemed like too much. He stared back, and there was a moment between us again. I held him there, fighting everything in me to stop myself from pulling him against me, hugging him, kissing him, and holding him tight.

I watched his breathing quicken, and I knew if I didn't move at that very minute, something was going to happen. Fear got the better of me, and instead of kissing him, I let my hands drop from his arms, and I looked at the snow.

"Damn. I left the salt in the back of the truck. I need to bring it in."

I hadn't. The salt was all in the barn where I needed it. But if I didn't get away from him at that moment, I wouldn't have been able to. I wasn't ready for that just yet.

Chapter Eleven
Matt

I left Dean to it. It was getting cold with the door open, and I still had work to do on the book. I closed the door behind him, made myself a coffee as he messed about in the increasing snowfall, and went back to my laptop.

Five minutes later, he was standing in front of the fire, looking at me. "You should probably charge your laptop and phone. I've just plugged my tablet in, but if the power goes, you'll want to keep working, right?"

I nodded and made a move to plug in my MacBook as he suggested.

I watched him warming himself and tried not to think about how close we had come earlier to doing something more.

I'd wanted it. I'd needed him to close the distance between us. Instead, he had made an excuse to head off and not make a move. I was disappointed. I understood it, but I was still disappointed. Something was brewing, and I wanted to know what was going to happen.

I sat there looking out at the snow, listening to the wind howl around the roof of the farmhouse, and pondering the future of my characters. I emailed my first five chapters to my editor while I had the chance; I needed her feedback to see if I was along the right lines.

Aside from the occasional crackle from the fire and the tapping of my fingers on the keys, there were no other sounds from inside the house. Outside, the wind whipped around and the snow fell more and more, blanketing everything, drifting in the blustering winds, swirling and dancing around in the fading light.

It was early evening and almost complete darkness when I finally got restless. My stomach growled, and I decided it was time for food.

I closed my laptop and let it finish charging. There wasn't anything else I was willing to do that day. My brain was distracted, and I wasn't sure I was writing anything that would be of any use to anyone. I sat in the quiet, staring out into the darkening surroundings, and the never-ending snowfall and wind.

Just as I was about to head into the kitchen, my mobile phone rang. I glanced at the screen; it was my editor. Shit.

"Hello?" *She couldn't be done with those chapters already, could she?*

"Babe! How are you? Listen, just calling about the chapters you sent through."

"Yeah?" I readied myself for the impending disaster. I honestly didn't think she was going to like them.

"They were amazing! Just what we were looking for. I hope everything is going well for the rest of it."

"It is." I bit my lip, holding back my sigh of relief.

"Listen, I don't want to keep you back from getting it finished. I just wanted to make sure you know it's all good, and to keep going. Okay, babe?"

I nodded and agreed with an 'uh-huh', and when she

was gone, I let out a long sigh. I had been worried sick that she was going to tell me she hated it. I was nervous I would have to start over and do it another way again. I really didn't think I had it in me for that.

When I got into the kitchen, the lights flickered. Shit. A moment later, Dean was at the door.

"Are you okay?" he asked as he came into the kitchen.

"I'm very good. Relieved, in fact. I just had my editor on the phone. She loved the chapters I sent her. The direction the book is heading in is good, and she's liking the character changes and all that. So, I'm delighted right now."

"I'm pleased for you." He smiled at me. "I was about to start cooking. Are you hungry?"

I thought about it. Someone else cooking for me was a far better idea than me trying to sort something out for myself. I nodded. "Starving. That's actually why I'm in here."

Dean grinned and started to busy himself in the kitchen. Soon, the smell wafting around was terrific. We were sitting around the same table we had had lunch at, but this time, there were candles on the table, ready for the lights to die.

"Oh, wow. This looks fantastic," I said when Dean put a plate down in front of me. "I didn't know you could cook like this!"

He shrugged with a small smile. "A man has to have some skills." There was a slight smirk, and I felt the under-tone of his words. My mind wandered to what other skills this man could possibly have, and I'm sure I was blushing when, in an instant, we were both distracted by the lights flickering.

"Shit. I think that's the power trying to tell us something," he said, setting his fork on his plate and lighting the candles on the centrepiece of the table. No sooner had he lifted his fork when the lights flickered again.

"The power really is going to go out then," I thought out loud.

Dean looked up at the light hanging from the ceiling. "It's looking like it."

I set my fork down and headed for the bathroom with a *back in a second*. Of course, it was then it happened. A slight flicker of the lights again and then darkness. "Crap," I exclaimed to the black around me.

"You okay in there?" I heard Dean call out from the other side of the door after a minute or so.

"I'm fine. I'll be out in a minute!"

Talk about embarrassing.

"I'm going to leave you a candle outside here on the table, okay?"

I could see the faint glow under the door.

"Thank you," I called out, and held my breath, waiting to see if I could hear him moving away from the bathroom door. Once convinced he was no longer lurking outside, I allowed myself to finish, washed my hands, and opened the door. Dean was nowhere to be seen, but the candle he had talked about was sitting right where he said it would be.

I went back down the hallway and into the kitchen, setting the candle back on the table with the others. "Thank you for that." I smiled at him as I sat down and resumed eating the delicious meal he had prepared for us.

There was definitely something about sitting with someone you were getting more and more annoyingly attracted to, eating a meal by candlelight. It was more than a little bit romantic. We sat there once again, in this awkward silence that seemed to taunt us every chance it got. It sat there between us, reminding us of all the things we couldn't manage to say to each other, and how much potential there was between us, and how much was being left unsaid.

Chapter Twelve
Dean

I was pleased Matt was enjoying the meal I had cooked for us because I wasn't so sure he was going to like my next suggestion all that much.

"Since the power's off, the heating system will be too," I announced, hoping he would, in some way, guess what I was going to say next. His blank expression told me otherwise. Fuck. "I would feel better if you stayed in the living room with me. It has the biggest fireplace. We can keep it burning through the night, and we can stay warm that way."

I waited for his reaction. "In the living room, *with* you?"

"It's the best way for us to keep warm, I'm afraid. I can keep it going during the night, and it's easier to do that with one fire than two."

"Oh, okay. I guess I can do that."

After dinner, Matt did the dishes with one of the heavy-duty torches. While he was busy, I gathered the extra quilts and comforters I had brought up with me for the other bedrooms. With that sorted, I headed back to the kitchen. "I'm going to make hot chocolate. Want one?"

Matt smiled and agreed. "Have you got mini marshmallows?"

I smirked. "As a matter of fact, I do." I remembered him liking them just as much as Finn did, and I always had them on hand because of that.

We took our mugs of liquid heat and headed back to the living room. Matt smiled at the amount of quilts and pillows on the floor and sofa. "Kinda reminds me of what your mum's living room looked like when Toni and I stayed at yours for the night."

I laughed and looked around; he wasn't wrong. We sat on top of the sofa with a few blankets around us and chatted about pure, innocent bullshit while we sipped our cocoa. How long did we think the snow would last? How long would the power be out? How long he'd been writing, and it was all so very natural with him. When we were both done with our mugs, Matt headed to the bathroom to get ready for the night, and I took the cups back to the kitchen.

When I finally got back to the living room, Matt was snuggled in under the covers on one end of the sofa. I put another log on the fire, made sure the guard was in place, blew out the candles, and parked myself at the other end of the sofa.

"I'll try to keep my hands to myself," I whispered in the dim firelight.

"Oh, okay," he whispered back.

Was he disappointed? Did he want me to touch him?

"I can't promise you won't wake up and find me snuggling in though."

I heard the smile in his voice, and he chuckled a little. "Okay. I think I can deal with that."

Oh, so can I, Matt. So can I.

When I woke the next morning, I was indeed snuggled up with Matt, but this was more on him than me. I thought about moving and uncurling myself from where he had his arm over me and his head on my chest, but I thought better of it. I liked having him there. Hell, I wanted more of having him there.

Instead, I chose to lie there in the silence and enjoy his warmth and his delicious scent against my body. It felt good to have him against me like that. It felt like he had always been destined to be right where he was at that moment.

I was just dozing off again when he stirred beside me, stretching, and creeping in closer. I didn't want the moment to end, but I knew it would soon when he realised fully where he was and what he was doing. His leg went over my thigh and slid up to my crotch. I knew that, when he was aware of where he was, he would also be very aware of the fact that I was lying there with him in my arms, and my cock was hard and ready for more.

I knew the exact moment he was aware of where he was too. I felt his body stiffen, and his leg moved away from mine.

He cleared his throat. "Morning," he murmured softly, pulling back from me already.

"Morning. Did you sleep well?"

He moved away from me, and I didn't like it. "Yes, uh, thanks." He was already getting out from under the covers and off the sofa. "I need to go to the little boys' room." He excused himself and headed out the door. I lay there, staring at the ceiling.

Fuck, I wanted more of Matt. I needed it. This was going to be almost impossible. The longer I lay there alone, missing the touch of him, the more I convinced myself that the only way through this was to make sure he didn't have to end up like this for the second time.

Yeah, like that would work in the middle of a nightmare snowstorm.

Chapter Thirteen
Matt

"You know, the fire and the Aga feed a hot water system. So you can have a shower if you want to," Dean told me.

"Really? That would be awesome. Thank you." I smiled at him, grateful I would be able to get myself feeling a little more human.

"You can also set yourself up to work in the kitchen at the table if you like. The Aga has the room nice and warm."

I smiled and hoped it wasn't being suggested because I had been neglecting myself while writing and stank a little. "Thanks, Dean. I really appreciate that."

I took myself to the bathroom and let the warm water help me. I was horny as hell. I let my hands roam over my skin. I needed more, I wanted more, and waking up that morning with the smell of him in my nostrils, and him very obviously turned on, it took everything I had not to touch him more. But I knew that, realistically, his hard cock probably wasn't even for me. It was just one of those naturally occurring things in the morning. Mine, on the other hand, had been very much about him. Thankfully, he didn't notice, or at least he never mentioned it.

My soapy hands continued to roam over my skin, thinking about what I would have liked to have happened that morning. How hard Dean had been. And while I wasn't exactly in the best position to find out, he certainly felt like he wasn't disappointing in the penis department.

My fingers teased my nipples, with the other hand holding onto my cock firmly, stroking it slowly. A moan escaped from me, and I bit my lip, worried Dean would hear me and I would make even more noise. Fuck, it felt so good to slide my fingers over the length of my cock and think about Dean. He had smelt incredible that morning. It didn't take long to work myself up to the brink of orgasm. I cupped my balls and let my hand settle into a strong clasp around my dick, the soap acting as lubricant, and I came hard, almost collapsing to my knees as my legs gave way with the power of my climax.

When I walked back into the kitchen, I was greeted with the smell of bacon and fresh coffee. "Oh, wow. It smells so good in here."

Dean was standing at the range, cooking. "I thought you might like breakfast." He smiled at me.

I was touched by his thoughtfulness. "Thank you." I smiled as he set a plate down in front of me.

"I've already had mine. I'm going to work in the house because of the weather. You'll have to tell me if you're annoyed by my noise."

I nodded. It was going to be harder to work on a book with no power, but at least I knew my MacBook had good enough battery life that I could get away with reading a chapter, then closing the Mac, and starting with my pen and paper. I would need to type it up later, but I could use my dictation software through that and self-edit as I went too.

Dean hovered around in the kitchen for a while as I finished the breakfast he had made for me.

"Have you had to deal with weather like this before?" I asked. He seemed to be a well-oiled machine in that respect, knowing just what to do.

"Once or twice," he admitted. "Em has some pretty remote properties. I was flooded in once, in Cornwall."

"Wow. On your own or with Finn?" My curiosity was piqued.

Dean collected my empty plate and started to wash it. "Just me. The boy was with his mum at the time."

I thought about it. Dean could have been hurt or worse, and I didn't like that idea, not one little bit.

"I'm glad you got through it safe and sound," I said.

He smiled warmly. "Ah, you can't get rid of me that easily. I'm going to go and try to get more work done now. Let me know if you need anything, and there's more coffee in the pot."

"Thanks, Dean. I really appreciate it." And with that, I was left alone with my thoughts and my book to work out my lust.

Chapter Fourteen
Dean

I was working on the far side of the house from Matt. There wasn't much I could do in the weather with no power or heat, but I was keeping busy inside while the weather didn't allow for much else.

There was noise somewhere in the house, and I stopped in my tracks and listened more carefully. As soon as I realised what it was, I started to laugh.

"Is that...?" I asked myself and stood in the doorway. I could hear Matt singing to himself from the kitchen.

He clearly had my headphones on again. I smirked. It was cute, and the song he was singing was one I had introduced him to years before. They had been my favourite band at the time. I liked that he still knew it and was singing it even now.

Before long, it was night time again, and we had spent time over dinner chatting again and having a pleasant evening.

Matt glanced over at me. I knew what he was thinking about.

"Ready to retire to the living room again?"

"Um, sure. Okay." He was keeping something to himself, and I wasn't about to try and pry it out of him. Instead, we sat talking again, telling more and more of the years we had lost touch.

We chatted until Matt admitted he was sleepy. I simply nodded and he went to get ready for bed.

Once Matt was finished in the bathroom, he appeared in the doorway of the living room as I sat on the sofa. "Are you sure you're okay about letting me sleep in here?" He smiled meekly.

"Of course!" I said, patting the seat beside me. He moved towards me and sat down.

"Thanks, Dean." He smiled at me.

"How's the book going?" I asked, needing to distract him and myself from the lack of distance between us.

"Well, it's a little longer of a process now I'm writing it by hand with the power out, but it's coming along nicely."

"Are your characters still hating each other?"

He smirked. "They are, but they have chemistry, you know. It's not just a plain loathing, it's more that they're hot for each other, but they're in a situation where that isn't allowed, so that just creates sparks and fire between them. They're learning more and more about each other as they go, and it turns out that they might actually like each other. Know what I mean?" Matt smirked and gestured with a tiny pinch.

I smiled, and I couldn't take my eyes off his handsome face, looking ethereal in the candlelight. "Oh, I know exactly what you mean."

Dammit, I didn't mean to come on so strongly, but I just

couldn't resist him. There we were sitting on the edge of a sofa, gazing at each other in candlelight. He was asking if I knew what it was like to be in lust with someone I shouldn't have been when all I wanted was him. I had never wanted to kiss someone so much in my entire life. He was addictive, and I wanted more.

He closed his eyes and sighed softly. His hand brushed against mine and I felt my cock hardening. He was far too easy to be comfortable around. He smelled so good, and the temptation to break all the rules that we had as kids was overwhelming.

"Well, I should probably get to sleep myself." I smiled.

He nodded, and without even thinking about what the hell I was doing, I leaned in and kissed his forehead. The air around us was crackling when I pulled back. I stared at him, and he stared at me. I didn't get to think about it too much before he crushed his mouth against mine.

Fuck.

I pulled him against me and returned his kiss hard. This was something I had waited a very long time for, and I wasn't about to pass up the opportunity. We kissed each other hungrily. His tongue lapped over mine, encouraging it to plunder his mouth. Christ, I was so turned on and hard it was painful.

"Jesus, Matt." I moaned against his lips as we paused to catch our breath.

He looked at me, startled. "Oh, shit. Dean, I'm sorry, I…"

I crashed my mouth back against his. Oh, no. No way was he going to apologise for kissing me and try to back out of it. I needed more, and I wasn't about to let him regret what this was. He pressed himself against me, responding with a passion comparable to my own, until, suddenly, he pushed me back.

"Dean, we can't," he panted against my face.

I got it. But I didn't want to. "It's okay." I nodded.

It wasn't okay. I wanted him, and now I knew he wanted me, but I presumed that because of all our previous history, and because of how complicated my life was, he couldn't act on it.

"I just…"

"You don't need to explain, Matt. It's honestly fine."

He nodded. He knew I was lying. I didn't know why he wanted me to stop, but I wasn't about to be an asshole to him.

I'm not sure how, but I made it to sleep without looking at him again, or taking him in my arms and insisting he needed to be with me, that I wasn't going to take no for an answer.

Chapter Fifteen
Matt

I really don't know what the fuck I was thinking. The man I had lusted after for so damn long was kissing me back like his life depended on it, and I somehow thought it would be better to just push him away.

Am I insane? Have I lost my mind?

No, I didn't think I had. I thought I was being respectful. I thought it was the right thing to do considering he had a child, and he didn't want to have a string of 'this is daddy's new boyfriend' men traipsing through his life. I'd been there. Every few months, my mother would bring home her latest 'love of her life' and I would have someone else to learn how to be around. I respected that Dean didn't want that for Finn.

It took everything I had not to catch him by the hand and pull Dean back towards me. To do everything I had dreamed of as a teenager, and everything that had crossed my mind over the last week or so that I had been in his company.

I wanted him, but it needed, for Finn, to be more. I didn't know if that was something Dean wanted.

I lay there in the darkness, with just the flicking of the fire for light, and thought about how I might just have made a big mistake in pushing him away.

The next morning, the snow had finally stopped. Dean found me working feverously at the table, lost in my words. When I looked up, I found him watching me work.

"Hey." He smiled warmly.

I looked up at him with a smile. "Hey yourself."

"It looks like the snow has stopped for a while. Do you want to get some fresh air? You've been working hard on that book."

I thought about it for a moment and then dropped my pen into the middle of my notepad and closed it. "God, yes! Getting outside to stretch my legs properly would be awesome. Where have you in mind?"

"Well, there's a great view of Ullswater and the surrounding mountains from the top field if you're game for it?"

I wasn't sure it was really the weather to go too far, but I trusted Dean, and I had been sitting in the house absorbed in my book for far too long. A little walk in some fresh crisp air would be just what I needed to refresh myself and come back ready to write more.

"Lead the way," I said, getting up from my chair and walking towards him.

Chapter Sixteen
Dean

I KNEW NOT to venture too far out from the farmhouse and the field or two around it. The snow was too deep, and it was damn cold, but even from the end of the lane, the view over Ullswater was good, so I knew that from the top field it would be even better.

Thirty minutes later, we were standing in the top field. I had been right. The view out over the lake and surrounding hills was more than picture postcard perfect. Matt stood there, watching out over the water, admiring the scenery, while I stood there admiring him. I loved to study him when he forgot anyone was looking. I enjoyed watching his mind churning as he looked around. I would have bet he was thinking about the kinds of people who had stood looking at the same scenery over the years. I knew he probably had his writer's mind working overtime with ideas already.

I was feeling a little playful though. He was getting too lost in his thoughts, and I wanted to bring him back to reality. Back to me. The clouds were coming back down over the mountains he was looking at, and I knew it wouldn't be long before the snow was back on again and we would have to head back. I crouched down while he was distracted, balled up a pile of snow between my hands, and aimed it squarely at his shoulder.

The snowball hit its target and broke upon impact in a spectacular explosion of white. He yelped in shock initially, but quickly realised what was happening when I launched a second snowball at him.

"Oh my God, you are so dead!" He laughed, stooping low to gather a ball of his own. His aim was lethal; his snow-ball slapped me right in the side of the face.

I glared at him. "Oh, is that how it is? Right, this means war!" I shouted, running back from him to gather more snow and launching it in his direction. The snowballs were flying through the air, and we were both having so much fun that I didn't realise how close we had crept to the ditches at the edge of the field.

There was a yell, and Matt disappeared from sight. I waded through the snow as quickly as I could to where his voice was coming from. When I arrived, he was flat on his back, covered in snow everywhere. I held out my hand to help pull him up out of the snow and the dip in the ground, but somehow, I lost my own footing and ended up smack bang in the snow alongside him.

"Fuck." I laughed, looking up at the snow-filled sky as more flakes started to fall. I pulled myself out of the ditch. I was covered in snow, and it was melting into my clothes with my body heat, making me cold. I steadied myself better this time and stretched my hand back out to Matt to pull him out.

I pulled him with such a yank that he slammed right

into my chest. His hands grabbed my arms to steady himself. For a moment, he stared at me.

Why the hell not?

I swiftly crushed my mouth on his. He kissed me back, squeezing my arms where he was holding on to me. In a few moments, he was shivering against my lips.

"We need to get back to the house before we freeze." I smiled and pulled his hand, pulling him as quickly as I could back to the warmth of the farmhouse.

We burst into the door, freezing and shivering. I kept pulling Matt along with me until we arrived in the living room in front of the fire.

"Are you okay?" I asked.

He shivered as he replied. "Yeah. I'm just a bit cold."

"Strip now," I demanded.

He looked at me like I had lost my mind.

"You heard me, Matt. You don't have time to argue. You're going to get hypothermia."

I started to strip myself off too.

"What are you doing?" He asked, his teeth chattering together as I ran my hands over my boxers. *Nope, they're wet too.* I started to shove them down my hips.

"We're going to share body heat."

"What?" Matt shook his head but still kept pulling off items of clothing.

"They're wet. We need to take off everything that's wet, and we need skin on skin contact to conserve what little body heat we have left."

Matt pulled off his soaked t-shirt, then pulled his boxers down his legs. I had wanted to get him naked, but this wasn't exactly how I thought it would transpire. I grabbed the quilt from the sofa, wrapped it around me, and pulled him into my lap on the floor in front of the fire. My front was to his back, his ass directly over my cold and flaccid cock. It wouldn't be staying like that once the heat started to get back into my body, I knew that much.

"Get your feet under the quilt," I ordered.

Matt pulled his feet in under the quilt and curled up, leaning into me. He sat there shivering on my lap, and all I could do was try not to think too much of the situation that I now found myself in.

His arms around me felt better than I ever thought possible. His skin on my skin, cold as mine was, was also bliss. I let myself lie there against him, drinking in the warmth of his body, letting him get some heat back into me.

Chapter Seventeen
Dean

I couldn't believe we had been so silly. Matt really could have gotten hypothermia, and we would never have been able to get him to a hospital. Telling him to strip and getting in under a quilt with him was the only thing I could think of that would help.

I didn't think it through, and I didn't anticipate the situation I found myself in. Matt on my lap, naked, my arms around his waist, his body pressed against mine. I could smell his aftershave and body wash, and it was all having an effect on me. I could feel the heat returning to his skin, and I knew that soon enough he would be okay.

I rested my head against his as he leaned it on my chest. I kissed the top of his head. Contented to have him here like that. Contented that he felt like he belonged there. He shivered against me, and I tried to think of anything that would stop my body from reacting the way it was.

When he looked up at me, I was a goner; the temptation of him was just too much. I slid my hand up over his chest to his neck and pulled his mouth to mine. I expected hesitance after the night before, but was greeted with none. His soft, full lips brushed over mine, his hands reaching behind him to my waist, kneading into my skin, and he pressed his body even tighter against mine.

I thought about all the times as a teenager I had wanted to do this with him. This was more than I could ever have imagined it would be. Matt shifted himself in my lap, straddling me. He ran his hands up my sides, over my shoulders, and cupped my face. I wasn't as sweet with my hands; I ran them down his back until I had a handful of arse in each one. I growled against his mouth softly, pulling his hips, grinding his cock and balls against my own. Wanting more. Needing to be inside him.

No man had ever had me so damn worked up before. No one had ever tugged at me emotionally like he did. Matt Elwes was going to be trouble; he was going to be the death of me, and that death would be caused by excessive lusting.

I kissed him hard, my tongue rolling over his, the feeling of his hard, bare cock against my stomach only making me need more. Without warning, Matt started to push back from me and broke our kiss.

"I want this." He looked at me intently, and I knew he really did. "But I think it might have to wait until we're sure that neither of us has pneumonia."

I smirked. "You want to be with me?"

Matt leaned in and kissed me softly. "You know I do. But I also want clothes, and heat, and to have our first time in a bed." He grabbed the comforter that was beside us, wrapped himself up in it, and disappeared off to the bedroom where some of his clothes here, leaving me with something to cover my rock-hard *modesty*.

Five minutes later, Matt was back, fully dressed, looking at me like he hadn't been fed in weeks and I was dinner. I wondered about when Matt had last been with someone. For me, it had been three years. Finn was about four years old when I stopped trying to have a relationship around him. I had a bad break-up. Finn had liked the guy and missed him not being around, and I realised it was time to forget about trying to get myself all loved up and worry about how it might all affect my son. It wasn't that I didn't want to date. It was just that I never really found anyone I wanted to be around like that. Maybe it was that I stopped looking. I wasn't sure, but yeah, it had been a while. And I hadn't been all that experienced to begin with, despite the reputation I'd had in secondary school. It was all stories. Things I told my straight friends to hide that I was gay and seem like this manly bloke to them. Christ, I really had been a moron back then.

"So, what do you think?" Matt asked, distracting me from my thoughts and making me realise I hadn't listened to a damn thing he had said.

"You didn't hear any of that, did you?" He smirked.

I raised an eyebrow. "No. Some naked bastard had me distracted."

"Did he, indeed? I'll have to have words."

I grinned. "Yeah, you do that. Tell him I'm looking forward to seeing him like that again as soon as I can."

Matt blushed. *Damn, that was sexy.*

"I will. In the meantime, what I said was, I'm going to make a stew, but I don't know if it's something you'll like. Is that okay?"

"If you make it with the pork sausages that are in the fridge, I think I might just love you forever, because that's how Finn's nanna makes it. Old Irish recipe passed down Jess's family, apparently, and it's bloody amazing."

Matt nodded. "Do you wanna go and get dressed, and I'll get started?"

I agreed and disappeared off to my room to find some clothes and try not to think of how much I wanted to be with Matt.

Chapter Eighteen
Matt

When Dean left the room, I finally let out the breath I'd been holding. I couldn't believe my luck. There I was being an idiot, probably making myself sick in the process, and Dean had spotted it and knew how to fix it. Plus, he really did need me as much as I needed him. I couldn't believe I was lucky enough to have another chance with him, an opportunity to *not* push him away this time, and to show him just what I thought of him.

I knew it was very early on, and that, aside from a kiss and a grope or two, nothing had really happened between us. But I felt like the intent for it was there, and not only that. It wasn't just lust. There was something else that felt like it was bubbling below the surface. Sure, it might just have been my imagination, and given that I was a romance writer, I did tend to let my mind run away into a flight of fantasy; but that wasn't what this felt like. Yes, I was nervous about it. Yes, I was worried about what he would want in return. But there was ultimately something else between us.

I thought more about what being with Dean would

involve. I knew he said he wasn't dating because he was worried about Finn's reaction to it all. Could the man really live his whole life like that? Worrying about what his son might think? Surely, he deserved to have a man who loved him and wanted to take on Finn with him. Would he want me to be that man? The more I thought about it, the more I wanted to be that man. Finn was an adorable child, and Jess seemed nice. I wondered if Dean would let me in and allow me to be part of the team they had for looking out for Finn. I wondered if Dean would let me be the one to look out for him too.

I snapped myself out of my overthinking and started to gather everything I needed for the stew.

After dinner, we were soon tucked up back on the sofa again. His hand met mine and our fingers intermingled.

"Thank you for today." I smiled at him.

"Thank *you* for the lovely meal."

I squeezed his hand a little more. "I mean it. I'm not sure why I didn't think about how stupid I was being by letting myself get so cold and wet."

Dean shook his head. "It happens. You're fine. It's not like you did it on purpose, and it's not like you actually got sick from it."

"But I could have, had it not been for you."

"But you didn't. And I wouldn't have let anything happen to you."

We both paused for a moment. He looked like he was thinking about whether he should elaborate or leave it at that. I looked at him as he glanced at me, and from the look on his face, I knew he didn't need to say any more than that.

There was a seriousness on his features that looked like he was considering the 'what-ifs', and that look made me feel like I needed to soothe him.

Without thinking about it any further, my mouth was on his. A soft, slow kiss that told him it was okay. That whatever had crossed his mind hadn't happened, wouldn't happen, and I was still right there with him and had no intentions of going anywhere.

He kissed me back with a touch of urgency, as though he was being careful not to work either of us up too much, and that was how we both left it. Soft, slow, and very sensual, but with an undertone of something more, until neither of us could keep our eyes open any longer.

Chapter Nineteen
Dean

We fell into the familiar pattern we seemed to have every night. One of us cooked, the other cleaned up. I sorted the fire, and we curled up together on the sofa. Matt still had his notebook and pen with him.

"How's the book going?"

He groaned and closed his pen in the notebook. "It's getting there, slowly. Just trying to decide what happens in the end."

I smiled. "Isn't that a given in romance? Isn't it always a fairy-tale ending with everyone living happily ever after?"

The look he gave me suggested he was surprised by how much I seemed to know about romance novels.

"Jess told me," I explained. "H-E-A. Right? Happily Ever After?"

He smirked. "Yes. That is indeed what they're meant to be having. I just can't figure out how."

"Want to talk it over?"

Matt shrugged. "Sure. It's just that they've just got together, and everything was very lust-fuelled and fast, and

I don't know how to turn it from that to their happy ending."

"Didn't you have all this sorted in the first version you sent to your editor?" I asked curiously.

"Kinda. It was a little messy, and with the extra parts I've put in now, it feels messier still."

"Okay, so tell me what you would like to see happen. Do they end up as a couple?"

He nodded.

"You have your drama already in there, right? Is that coming back to bite them?"

He shook his head with a frown. "No. I don't think it is."

"So, what's the problem?"

He opened the book and flicked through it absently, trying his best not to make eye contact. Suddenly, I realised this wasn't about his book at all. It was about us, and he was probably too damn distracted to write because of us.

"What if it's the intense situation they're in, and it's that which has made them like this? All over each other. All seeming loved up."

And there we had it. "You're worried that once everything is back to normal, they'll realise it was a mistake and stop?" I asked.

He glanced at me sheepishly from the corner of his eye. "Yes." He closed his eyes and continued. "What if they think it's all wonderful now, but once they get back into the real world, they come to the conclusion that they aren't as compatible as they thought. That they were in lust and not love, and it all ends."

"I'm not going to think that," I insisted.

Matt's eyes widened, and he stared at me, stuttering. "No, I didn't mean... I mean, I was just talking about..."

"Us," I interrupted.

"No. I mean, maybe. I mean, oh fuck…" His voice trailed off in defeat. He had managed to tie himself in knots.

I reached for his hand, took the notebook from him, and set it on the end table behind where we were sitting. I took his hand in mine and smiled at him, touching his cheek softly.

"I know this situation isn't average, or in any way conventional. I know there are things that haven't been done, haven't been said, and a lot of things that need to be talked about. But this isn't just being horny for you and misreading signals," I explained.

"You were my teenage crush, for fuck's sake."

I grinned. I couldn't help myself. I had a good idea that was the case back then, and I had felt the same about him, even if I had been a self-denying wanker who never acted on it. "And you were mine."

He looked at me like I'd just told him the biggest lie he'd ever heard.

I shook my head. "Don't you dare think it's not true. You weren't in my head back then. You don't know what I thought about when I was alone with my cock in my hand. You don't know how I watched you be yourself, and out and proud, and think about how much I admired you even more for that. I didn't admit to myself I was gay back then, but I did admit to myself that I liked you, a lot."

He tried to defend his fears, but I wasn't having it. "No. You're not going to talk yourself out of it. I've seen you do that in the past, and while I'm very glad you did because I kind of like where we've ended up now, I don't want you to do that here."

Matt held his finger on my lips to stop me from talking more. "I know it's a big ask to let me into your life with Finn, and I know he has to come first. That's why I worry.

That's why I'm thinking about it all carefully. Because, honestly, Dean, I've never felt like this about anyone. Not then, and not now. I've been single over the last few years. It's one of the reasons my career is doing as well as it is, because I've had the time for just me, and to do whatever I needed to for my success. And I know that means travelling. I know that means stress and deadlines and everything else, and I know that isn't something that makes a relationship easy, especially not with a child in tow."

"You don't think if it's as simple as two people loving each other, that's enough?" I asked, without thinking of what I was really admitting to.

Matt's eyes widened. "Are you saying what I think you're saying?"

I shrugged. Too late to hide it now. "Maybe."

He didn't say anything else. He kissed me, and not the soft kiss we had had the night before. This was raw. This was full of passion and everything that had been unspoken over the last however many years it had been since we first admitted to ourselves that we liked each other. Lust, wanting, needing to be with the other poured out. I pulled back from him, took him by the hand, and stood, pulling him up with me.

"Where are we going?"

"The bedroom," I told him.

His face went red, and silently, he followed me.

Chapter Twenty
Dean

I HADN'T WANTED to drag someone to my bedroom for a very long time. But I knew if I didn't do it there and then with Matt, he would overthink it all to death before we'd even started. I needed to prove to him how good it would be between us, and it wasn't just a passing fling; it was something real and meaningful.

We got to the bedroom with our candle, and I closed the door. The firelight and the candle were enough to allow us to see each other and cast a romantic glow over us.

I brought the hand I was still holding to my mouth and kissed over his knuckles. He watched every move I made as I did it. I pulled him against me, wrapping my arms around him and encouraging him to wrap himself around me.

I didn't want to lose the contact between us, so I moved Matt back towards the bed, putting my knee between his legs as I did. When I came to a stop, we were both on the bed, with him beneath me, and me right where I wanted to be; between his thighs.

He looked at me tenderly and caressed my face, his fingertips leaving a trail of energy coursing through my skin.

I could have easily melted into his touch with the tenderness he was showing me. No matter what else happened, I wanted this man; he was the other half of my soul. I knew he might not feel the same. I knew it might all one day go to hell. I knew it, and I didn't care. He was always going to be worth the risk to me.

I pressed my mouth against him and claimed him with a soft kiss, and when I rolled my hips against him, right where he needed me most, that kiss devoured his delicious sounds too. I was going to take my time. I was going to enjoy this. We lay on my bed, enjoying the teasing and foreplay that was us effectively dry humping like a couple of frisky teenagers. Only this was going to be so much more.

His hand slid under my t-shirt, tickling me as it stroked over my skin. My cock throbbed at the thrilling touch of his skin on mine again, and I needed more. I pulled back from him, whipped the t-shirt over my head, and sank back down to kiss him firmly. My heart thundered in my chest, and I flexed my hips against him, my cock so in need of being buried inside him. His legs came up around my hips, locking me between his strong thighs. I mirrored the movements of his hands and slid one of mine under his top, sliding over all his glorious chest hair, finding his nipple pebbled and rubbing over it with my fingertips.

His back arched against me, and his mouth vibrated against mine as he moaned in want. I didn't know which of us I was teasing more. I was suddenly very grateful for the wank I had that morning, so I wasn't making a complete idiot of myself.

I knew one thing; he had too much covering his body. Not enough of it was free for me to admire. I pulled back from him and shoved his jumper over his body. He knew what I needed and finished taking it off for me. I stared. I couldn't help myself. He was stunning. His skin glowed in the light from the fire, his chest rising and falling rapidly in his sexual need, and his pebbled nipples jutting out through his glorious chest hair. I took advantage of the fact that I didn't need to support myself with the way I was sitting, and I stroked both hands along his sides, mapping my way over his ribs, and covered his pecs with my hands, kneading his flesh. The sensation was indescribable, finally touching what I had wanted to for so long. If I was dreaming, I really didn't want to wake up.

I lowered my mouth over a nipple. He gasped and whimpered all at once, and I started to suckle at his flesh hungrily. My tongue rolled over the sensitive skin of his chest, drawing a series of soft moans from him, my hands roaming all over him. I needed this man more than I need air, and I detached my mouth from his and looked at him like a wolf looking at prey.

"You have way too much on, and so do I," I told him, moving away and starting to strip off. Matt watched for a moment and then moved from the bed and mirrored my actions. His belt hit the floor, followed by everything else that had been covering his beautiful body.

He stood, naked, on the other side of the room, watching me as my cock sprang free from my jockey shorts. He was staring right at my cock, his mouth open in surprise, and I thought just how beautiful it would be to feel his mouth around my dick. *Mmm, that would do later.*

"Matt, if you keep looking at me like that, you're going to get it."

He grinned at me like that was some kind of challenge, his eyes not moving from my crotch. "Is that a promise?" He smirked.

Fuck, this man is incredible.

I raised an eyebrow at him. "Matthew," I warned.

His lips parted, and he stopped looking at my dick, letting his eyes roam over my body, all the way up to my face, letting his tongue snake out over his lips, leaving them glistening in the firelight.

Jesus.

I kneeled on the bed and beckoned him over with a crook of my finger. He obliged, and once he was close enough, I yanked him against me and flopped back down on the bed on top of him. My dick was pressed against his hip instead of where I wanted it, but I would remedy that soon enough. I gave him a light and playful kiss on the tip of his nose and then settled myself back to where I had been, my mouth hovering just over his nipple, breathing hotly over it, making him want it first.

"Dean," he pleaded, and I rewarded him with my mouth sinking over his sinfully beautiful chest. I rested on one elbow while I sucked on him and used my other hand to caress and tease his other nipple. His breathing quickened, and I realised just how sensitive my man's nipples were. *My man.* Fuck, I loved the sound of that. My tongue swirled over that little bundle of raw nerves, only stopping to suck it further into my mouth, teasing the other one between my finger and thumb.

He let out a low moan, and his body began to tremble. Jesus, I could feel how hard he was against my thigh. Every nerve in his body seemed to be primed and ready to explode, and fuck me, if I didn't want to take him there.

I licked over his nipple and stopped, and he looked down at me through hooded eyes. His usually sparkly brown eyes were almost inky black and gleaming with pure lust. I grinned. I liked that. I had a sneaking suspicion I was going to be addicted to seeing his face looking at me like that.

I positioned myself over him, pressed my knee between his thighs, and let him know just where I wanted to be as I pressed my lips to his and kissed him hard again. His legs and lips parted at the same time, allowing my body to come to rest between his thighs, and my tongue to lap over his.

My body lined up perfectly with his. I could feel and see just how hard he was, and it felt like my cock was going to burn up before I finally got it I needed it. Resting on one hand, the other caressed and teased his chest again, rolling his nipple between my finger and thumb. He groaned against my mouth and shifted his hips against me. My cock slid behind his balls and I could feel how we were almost perfectly lined up for me to sink right into him, but I held myself back. Christ only knows how.

Chapter Twenty-One
Matt

Lying beneath Dean was beyond anything I had ever imagined happening when I was a teenage boy. He had moved again and was now between my legs, his cock rubbing against my balls and teasingly nudging at my arse, and I was suddenly a little nervous about how I would react to him touching me anywhere else with anything else.

When he kissed me, and his hand skimmed over my skin to my chest again, I couldn't help but shift my hips against him. I wanted more. I needed more, and all this slow and tender was only setting the bar higher and higher for when he finally sank inside me.

I was so turned on, my cock had leaked all over my stomach. It throbbed, and already I ached to come. I could feel how hard he was, and I wanted nothing more than to have him move the tiniest fraction more and let his cock slide right in where it was meant to be. There was very little keeping us apart; there was very little keeping me holding on to my sanity.

Again, he twisted my nipple, and I couldn't take it anymore. "Please, Dean," I pleaded.

He looked at me, wet his hand with his spit, and rubbed it over his cock and my arsehole.

"Do it," I begged, and his perfectly aligned cock slid slowly just where I wanted it to be. He pried his mouth from mine and moaned out. "Oh, fuck, Matt."

I thought he might stop himself; instead, he pushed back against me and didn't stop until every inch of his magnificent dick was firmly enshrouded in the tight warmth of my needy arsehole.

When he pulled back and slid all the way back in again, I cried out. The sensation was better than anything I had ever experienced before. No man would ever feel like this inside me. Not ever. He grabbed my ankles and put them over his shoulders. I rocked my hips up to meet his every move as he started a slow and steady pace, sliding into me as deeply as he could over and over.

The man wasn't fucking me. He was making love to me. It was perfect. It was beautiful. It was, I realised at that moment, something no man had ever done to me before in my life. I was twenty-eight years old, and not once in that time had I ever been more than someone to fuck.

I don't know how he managed to keep up the pace he did. I don't know how he resisted the temptation to get faster and drive into me harder. I wasn't complaining. Oh, I was moaning, but it was for a much different reason.

I wasn't thinking about what happened after. I wasn't worrying that this would all stop. I didn't care; those thoughts didn't even occur to me. It was all just Dean and me. Nothing else in the world existed.

Dean let my ankles slide from his shoulders and he dipped his head and pulled my nipple into his mouth again. Mixed with the tempo of his cock deep inside me, it had me hot and already so needy to come for him.

"Oh, Dean!" I cried out as slid his cock all the way back into me again.

He paused, buried inside me, and waited until I had been able to catch my breath before continuing. "You feel so good when you clamp down around my cock," he whispered across my lips before claiming another kiss.

I couldn't take it. I wrapped my legs around his waist, my feet resting on his arse as I crossed my ankles, trapping him. I hungrily ran my tongue over his, kissing him back as hard as I could. Because of my legs, he had no option but to start short, faster strokes, staying mostly within my warm depths. I grabbed at his arms. I squeezed his biceps. I ran my fingers over his chest and his back, staring at him, never letting him break the look that was being exchanged between us.

It felt so incredibly intimate to be looking right at someone as they repeatedly teased every nerve inside you and drove you towards a climax, but I couldn't look away. I didn't want to look away.

"That's it, Matt," he encouraged as he wrapped his hand around my cock. He dropped his head to my chest and covered my other nipple with his mouth, sucking on it lightly and encouraging me to orgasm. Every inch of me shuddered in a powerful climax as thick ribbons of my cum covered the space between us. I repeated his name over and over, like it was the only word I had the brain power to produce. I felt everything, everywhere. I was on overload, and I couldn't believe how incredible it felt.

Dean stilled inside me as he rode out the waves of my orgasm from within me. He glanced up at me and moved instantly from my chest back to my mouth. I became convinced he was actually trying to kill me. Slowly, he started to move inside me again. Every time he did, the next crest of pleasure came harder and faster than the one before it, prolonging my orgasm for as long as he could manage.

I have no idea how Dean kept going. Sweat covered him. His movements were getting less rhythmic. I knew he was finally getting close to his own climax. I put my hand on his cheek, and he looked right at me. From his cheek, my hand moved to the rest of his body, starting with his neck and shoulders, over his arms, grabbing his biceps.

He had been inside me so long that, with his cock hitting against that little bundle of nerves inside me, I could feel yet another orgasm building, and I wanted this one to take Dean over the edge with me. I kept gazing at him. I kept stroking him and grabbing him. His hand came up and cupped my face, and he looked at me like I was the most precious thing he had ever seen.

The next words out of my mouth surprised even me. Of all the dirty things I could have whispered, of all the filthy encouragement I could have uttered, only one phrase came from my mouth when he looked at me like he was.

"Oh, God, Dean. I love you."

Dean's breathing hitched, and he looked right at me as he and I finally came together. His arms wouldn't hold him up anymore, and still inside me, he fell forward, the full weight of him leaning on my body. I didn't want him to move. I didn't want him to pull out. I wrapped my legs back around him, wanting to keep him right there for as long as I could.

Tears started to spill from the corners of my eyes. I held my breath to prevent myself from crying and Dean thinking he had done something wrong. He hadn't. The tears falling from my eyes were the tears that happen when you realise you've been missing out on something for such a long time. When you understand that nothing you have ever felt will come close to how you feel in that moment.

He nuzzled into my neck. "I love you too, Matt. I always have."

I couldn't hold it back at that point. A strangled sob escaped from me. Dean's head and shoulders shot up instantly to look at me. How could I explain this?

Dean smiled at me and kissed me softly. "You don't need to cry, sweetness. It's okay. I've got you." His kind words soothed me. He wiped my tears and kissed my face.

"I just..." I started to explain.

"Shhh. I know. Hits you hard, doesn't it?"

He got it. I didn't need to explain. I didn't need to tell him what I was thinking. He just understood.

Chapter Twenty-Two
Dean

As HE LAY there in the darkness, curled in against me, almost asleep, I felt like all my dreams had come true. Of all the words that could have fallen from his lips at that moment, the only ones he found were of love. Matt Elwes loved me.

I closed my eyes, drinking in the scent of him, feeling him pressed against me, my arms around him, and I let sleep claim me like I had just claimed Matt.

The next morning, Matt still slept. I set about making a light breakfast for us and headed back to my bedroom.

"So, that's where you were." Matt smiled at me, stretching out on the bed when I came back into the room.

"I thought you might need some food after using all that energy last night." I grinned at him.

"Did something happen last night?" He grinned back, teasing me.

I smirked. "Shit, am I in the wrong room again? My

boyfriend must still be down the hall." I went to get up and move away from him, but he grabbed my arm and pulled me back to him.

"Uh, no, mister. I think you found your boyfriend right here." He beamed back.

I moved my mouth closer to his. "Oh, did I now? My boyfriend, you say?"

He nodded, and that was all I needed. I leaned in and claimed his mouth for the first of many times with him as my boyfriend. I loved being able to call him that. I had waited a very long time.

My heart was full of hope, and my mind was full of ideas about what could come next between Matt and me. One thing was certain in my mind. I wasn't going to be single anymore. From the little I had seen of Matt interacting with my son, and Finn's reaction to Matt as he was leaving, I knew they would get along.

Outside, the snow had stopped falling, and the sun was shining; it was a picture postcard sight. I headed out to get more logs for the fire and to check everything over. Some of the farm buildings were in a serious state of disrepair, and I was worried the weight of the snow on them would bring their roofs down.

Matt had said he wanted to get a little more writing done. He said the words were flowing, and he didn't want to stop. He was scribbling away, mumbling to himself, with the occasional yearning breath escaping from him as he worked. I left him to it.

· · ·

When I got back into the farmhouse later, I glanced over. I saw him, slumped over his notebook, his pen fallen from his hand, sound asleep. "Matt?" I whispered as I approached him.

He moaned softly. Nope, this guy was well and truly asleep. I lifted his pen and notebook, skimming over the pages, smirking at the hot sex scene that had apparently been the reason for his moans.

I carefully lifted his shoulders from the desk. He barely stirred in his slumber, and I smiled. He looked so peaceful, and he was clearly exhausted from working hard on his book, not to mention some of the other activities he'd been doing a lot of the last few days.

I bent, placing the tenderest of kisses on his forehead before giving him a soft jostle to wake him up. "Matt. You can't sleep there, darlin'. It's not going to be comfortable."

"Okay," he mumbled. He let me help him to his feet, and half asleep, I walked him the few steps needed to get him on the sofa, where it was warmest.

I woke earlier than I needed to. The room was still partially lit by the diminishing glow emanating from the fireplace. Matt was tucked tightly against me, our bodies a tangled mess of limbs. His head rested on my chest, moved only by the rise and fall of it with every breath I took.

His thigh was draped over my legs, his foot between my knees as his knee was lined up with my cock, partially covering the morning wood I had been unable to avoid with such a glorious creature tucked in beside me. I absently stroked his hair as I watched him sleeping.

My touch made him subconsciously aware of my presence, and he snuggled in tighter. His arm pulled him against my side, his nose nuzzling against my chest hair, and God help me, his leg flexed and moved teasingly over the length of my cock. A low, rumbling moan vibrated through me.

His head moved, and his sensual mouth was suddenly against my chest, peppering it with feather-light kisses.

Oh, fuck. He's awake.

His hand slid over my skin. My breathing quickened, and he shifted his leg once again, another moan escaping my lips because of his agonising, teasing movement.

The sensation that crept over my skin made me shiver. Everywhere he touched me was the focal point of pleasure, and it felt like he was touching me everywhere. He knew just what he was doing. He moved against me again, his knee stroking over my dick. My hand slipped from his hair to his strong back, memorising the shape of him with my fingertips, fearing I would wake up and this would be all a dream.

His kisses got needier. I could feel that he was getting just as turned on by all the teasing as I was. The air around us was thick with lust and yearning. Matt's mouth found my nipple. A surge of pure energy coursed through my body from my nipple to the tip of my throbbing cock.

"Fuck, Matt!" I gasped, my hand on his head, holding him against my chest. Christ, he was driving me insane. He was making my need to be inside him greater with every single second he teased me and set my soul alight with lust.

His tongue flicked over one nipple, and his fingertips circled over the other. That was it; I just couldn't take it anymore. I slid my hand along his thigh to his cock and held him firmly, grabbing at him, needing him to shift his body against me and get on top of me. Instead, determined to draw it out just a bit longer, he looked up at me with an intensity that no one had ever looked at me with before. He ground his hardness against my hip. Fuck.

"Matt..." I growled, half warning, half begging.

Chapter Twenty-Three
Matt

I WANTED HIM. No, I needed him. When all this started, I had felt like a schoolboy with a crush, and an unrequited one at that. But as time had gone on, what I had ended up feeling was emboldened. I was more than I thought I could be to someone because the person I had wanted and lusted after for all my teen years was actually here. He was actually gay and really did fancy me back. But there was more depth to my feelings for my best friend's brother than him being the lad I had fancied for a few years. This was the man I was in love with. This was the man I needed to have around me in my life, body, and soul. Until then, I hadn't believed in soul mates, and during a freak snowstorm in the English Lake District, I had found that soulmates were indeed a very real thing, and I happened to have one.

Right then, I needed Dean. I had waited for the longest time for him. Ever since he had carried Toni piggyback from the old skate park where she had been showing off and took a tumble off his skateboard. He carried her back to their house as she cried snot bubbles down his back. He held her hand as his mum picked all the gravel out of Toni's broken, bleeding skin. He distracted her, told her jokes, anything he could to make her feel better. My heart fluttered for the first time at that moment, and I don't think it ever really stopped.

I avoided him on social media. I zoned out when he was mentioned, to the point where Emily stopped talking about him around me. I think Toni might have told her about my crush, as if she didn't already know, and she probably said to stop mentioning him. It was everything I had thought about for years. Hearing about him was just something more to torture me with, and I didn't need it.

But right then, things were very different. I needed him to make me feel better in a very different way. I needed him more than I needed air to breathe. An all-consuming desire to join with the man who held my heart was all I could think about. I rolled my hips and started to grind against him. With every ounce of wanting and desire, I needed him.

He looked at me, and my heart skipped a beat under the fiery intensity of his gaze. There was something smouldering, unsaid, beneath it. His hand grabbed at my thigh as I teasingly rubbed it along his length again. His other hand arrived at my other side, and he tried to push me, to encourage me to move so I was straddling him. God, the thought of him between my thighs made my dick throb, and I needed no further encouragement.

I released his nipples from my mouth and my fingers, and with minimal effort, Dean helped me climb on top of him. I kept my eyes on his and let my hands trail over my thighs, caressing my body, feeling that wild abandon that comes from feeling genuinely sexy in the eyes of the person you're with. I gasped as I ran my fingertips slowly over my stomach. I caressed my chest, skimming over the hair I had there, and bit my bottom lip, fighting a moan as I teased my nipples, all the while staring right at Dean.

I was rewarded with a twitch of his cock, right at the crack of my arse, making me groan more. I ran my hands back down my body and over my cock, rolling my hips and grinding against his hardness, needing so much more, but delighting in how much teasing he was letting me get away with.

His hands found my thighs, his breathing rapid, his hips flexing up against me. Goosebumps prickled over my skin at his touch as he traced his fingertips over me, along the path I had just teased him with. The sensation of his big hands cupping my pecs drove a moan from my throat. "Ohhh, fuck, yes." I gasped, my head falling back in exquisite pleasure.

His thumb and forefinger rolled over my nipples, tugging them. I was panting, needy, and breathless. I felt like the man could make me blow my load just with his touch, and the endless temptation of the hardness of his thick cock against my ass, yet not quite where it needed to be.

Dean pressed himself harder against my arse, and my head rolled forward to look at the man who was setting my body on fire. The intensity was still in his gaze, and his hands slid up to cup my face as he pulled me down to lie on top of him. His lips crushed against mine the moment I was close enough.

His arms wrapped tightly around me, and he devoured my mouth hungrily with his own. I pried my mouth from his and pushed back off his chest so I was sitting, looking at him.

"Dean," I begged him, pressing my needy ass against him.

"Are you sure you want this?" he asked, caressing my face.

I nodded. I had never been more certain of anything in my entire life.

His hand gripped my hips, and he ground his cock against my ass again, looking at me with a fire that I thought would make me disintegrate instantly. "You want this?" he asked again, putting a particular emphasis on the word by rubbing his dick against me once again.

"Yes!" I gasped.

Dean didn't hesitate; he spat into his hand, rubbed it over his length and held his cock in place as I moved and slid down on his impressive length. He gripped my hips to try and slow me. It just wasn't what I needed or wanted. Instead, I pushed myself down on him, needing him inside me, craving the feeling of him stretching out my needy hole. I needed him all, and I wasn't about to wait a single second more to get him.

Chapter Twenty-Four
Dean

I wanted to still him. I tried to slow him for even a second. I wanted to savour the feeling of his glorious fucking arse taking every inch of me inside. I wanted to memorise how it felt to finally get to where I had wanted to be for years. But he was just as needy to take all of me. At that moment, I realised he had been waiting for me for as long as I had been waiting for him.

"Oh, fuck, Matt!" I groaned as he settled himself on my balls, every inch of me buried deep inside him. This was perfection. There was no other word to describe it, and yet that word was contrite and nowhere near enough. I held his hips, caressing his skin under my hands, and I let him take everything he wanted to take from me.

Matt's hands found themselves on my pec muscles, his fingertips grazing over my nipples with every movement he made as he bounced himself up and down, fucking himself with my dick. I watched him; his smiles, his gasps, the way his eyes half closed, the way his back arched, how his mouth formed a pretty 'o' every time he took me to the fullest, slamming me deep.

The man rode me, and I watched the glorious show as he did. He took what he needed and got himself off on me several times. My cock hit the perfect spot inside him to make him come, and his cock leak milky juices. My cock twitched, and throbbed, and fucking ached. He was edging me, teasing me to the brink, and then letting the feelings slip back, only to start again when his own orgasm passed. It was too much. Every inch of me prickled with excitement and electricity I'd never experienced before. He was torturing me in the most delicious way. It was everything. Matt Elwes was everything.

I needed more. I needed to come right in that delicious ass of his before he had my cock too sensitive to do anything with it. I pulled him down against me and, holding his hips, rolled us, keeping my cock firmly inside him as I did.

I pulled out of him for just a moment, getting onto my knees between his legs, pulling his buttocks to rest on my knees. "You're going to pay for all that teasing, Matt." I grinned at him.

He beamed back at me, and I slid back inside him before leaning forward to kiss him with everything I had.

With Matt on his back, I was able to control the pace, and I was going to make sure this was sex he would never forget for the rest of his life. I rolled my hips against him, my hand over his cock as I did.

"Oh, fuck!" He gasped when he felt exactly what I was going to do to him.

"Mmmm. Feel that, Matt?" I said as I thrust into him again. "That's how much I need you. How much I love you. How much I always have." Every broken sentence was punctuated with a long, slow stroke deep inside him, all the while my hand firmly around his cock, the movements of my hand in perfect time with the movement of my hips.

He couldn't say anything in reply. I had taken his breath away with my words and my actions. I made love to him. I poured out everything I had ever felt for him, everything I had ever thought about him, years' worth of love expressed through the union of our bodies.

Matt finally gifted me with his glorious orgasm and caressed my back, face, and arms as I found my own release within him, those small actions telling me what he felt for me too. It was everything. And I knew that, even if the moment faded and what was happening never made it beyond a freak snowstorm in the Lake District of England, Matt Elwes would have no doubts that he was loved, and adored, and always would be.

We stayed there, intertwined with each other, cuddling, and basking in the post-sex glow.

"I feel like I've come home," he murmured against my chest.

My heart skipped a beat, and I pulled him tight against me. I felt it too, a thing I had never understood until right at that moment, lying there with Matt. People often said home wasn't a place, it was a person, and not until right there with him in bed beside me did I realise what that really meant.

"I think I'll keep you."

"You think?" I smirked.

He squeezed me tighter, and I heard him smile when he spoke. "I know I will."

I grinned. "I know I want to keep you too."

"You do?" He looked up at me.

If he still needed reassurance after everything that happened between us, I was only too happy to provide that.

I caressed his cheek, holding his gaze so he would have no doubts about my honesty. "I do. I love you, Matt."

Tears threatened to bubble from his eyes, and he buried his head back against my chest before he spoke. "I love you too, Dean."

I held him and stroked his hair as we dozed off again, contented in the love that surrounded us.

Chapter Twenty-Five
Matt

Sometimes I wondered if it was the passion that had been radiating out from the farmhouse the last few days, but the snow had finally stopped, and the temperature started to rise. About two days ago, the power came back on.

Dean and I had continued to share our love, and each other, and I don't think I'd ever been happier my entire life. My book was finished. I had been furiously typing out everything, catching up on all I had missed while the power was out.

I knew it sounded conceited, but I honestly thought that book might be my best one yet. I also thought a lot of that was down to the inspiration, passion, and romance Dean had been wrapping around me while I'd been there.

Just as I was typing up the last two chapters, Dean wandered into the living room, warming his gorgeous arse by the fire. I stopped for a moment to glance over at him as he rubbed the heat back into his buttocks. Damn, that was a sexy ass, and I needed to get my hands on it again soon.

His face looked a little forlorn.

I got up and moved over to stand in front of him, wrapping my arms around his waist. "What's up?"

His arms wrapped around me in return, and he just held me tight against him. "I think the snow's starting to thaw."

I was confused.

"You'll be able to escape soon. Head back to the big city and get on with writing more books. I'll bet Toni will have the cocktails ready the second you get back." He laughed, but there was something missing from it. It was trying too hard to be playful when all it really was was tinged with sadness.

I felt him squeeze me a little tighter. "Is that what you want? Do you want to head home?"

I shook my head. "Does it have to stop? Do we have to part ways?"

Dean looked at me. "Not if that's not what you want, Matt."

I looked up at him. "I love you," I told him. "I don't want whatever this is to stop."

"So, don't let it then. I want you too, Matt." He smiled and pulled me tight against him, snuggling against me. "I love you too," Dean admitted as he slid his hands around my waist.

I stood there, in the middle of a big old farmhouse, and I honestly couldn't think of a single place I would want to be more than where I was right then. Cherished, loved, and very much lusted after by my beautiful man.

"So, we'll figure it all out then?" he asked, his face in my shoulder.

I held him tight. "We will. This will work."

We looked at each other, and again, I felt that pull

towards him. This had to work. Dean was home, and I couldn't think of anywhere else I wanted to be.

I woke beside Dean with the sounds of my phone screaming on the bedside table. He grumbled behind me and pulled me in against him as I grabbed for my phone. "Hello?"

"Matt, darling! Did I wake you?"

My editor. Shit. "No. No, I was awake." Dean stirred again behind me. "Is everything okay with the book?" I was nervous. Initially, she had been excited about the book, but what if she was changing her mind?

Dean's lips met my bare shoulder, instantly distracting me from my worrying.

"No, babe. Everything is just fabulous. So fabulous, in fact, that we would like to send you on a book tour, starting next week. Do you think you could get yourself down here to London tomorrow and we can start going over the details?"

"What?" Leave the farm? Leave Dean?

"Look, get yourself in the car and get back to civilisation and we'll talk about it."

"How long will it be?"

"Well, initially we have plans for three months, with the possibility of an extension."

My heart sank, bypassing my stomach and landing right in my feet.

"Okay." I hung up, flicked my phone on to Do Not Disturb, and set it back on the bedside table.

"What is it?" Dean asked against my arm.

I didn't want to think about leaving him. I didn't want to think about the possibility of being away for at least three months. I rolled into Dean's embrace, and I kissed him hard. He wrapped his arms around me and pulled me tight against him.

He knew something was bothering me; he was trying to kiss my problems away. God, I wished it was possible, and I wished that what was wrong with me was actually a problem. I was successful. My book was going to be another hit. My publisher was delighted with my work and willing to invest in a book tour. That was huge. That was everything I wanted to achieve, yet as I thought again about leaving the man I had become so attached to, I just couldn't see it as a happy event.

"Are you going to tell me what's wrong?" he whispered against my lips. I couldn't look at him. "Matt, you're worrying me. What is it?" His thumb swept over my cheek.

"They want me to go on a book tour, to promote the book."

Dean grinned with pride. "But that's brilliant. That means they like it, and they're going to spend a lot to promote you, right?"

I nodded.

"So, how is that a bad thing? Why are you upset?"

"I have to leave tomorrow, and it's for at least three months."

His smile faded. "Ah."

"Now you understand?" I could feel my eyes prickle. I didn't want to leave. Not yet. Maybe not ever.

Dean caught my mouth with his again. "It's okay, Matt," he breathed against my lips. "I love you. You're not getting rid of me, even if you do have to go away to work for three months."

He tried to reassure me, and I loved him all the more for

it. I just wasn't sure if I could believe it would actually work out the way he thought it would.

His hands stroked tenderly and comfortingly over my body, turning me on and driving all my fears and doubts away. He kissed me tenderly, and I got lost in the feeling of his body against mine, his love pouring into me with his actions. I let him make love to me and drive away my anxiety for a while.

My editor called three more times that morning, just to find out when I would be back in London, when I wanted to start the book tour, and if I had the email she had sent me of the publisher's plans for me. I showed it all to Dean.

"I'm not sure I can do this." I sighed.

He took my hand in his. "I know this is very new, and I know long-distance relationships suck. But, Matt, I've been waiting for you for a fucking long time, and I'm not going to disappear on you now. Not even for a second. We can video call, we can text. I can get cheap flights and you can show me the sights of whatever town you're in next." He let his thumb trace circles over the back of my hand as he spoke, trying to reassure me with everything he had. This would work and everything would be okay.

Chapter Twenty-Six
Dean

I DIDN'T KNOW what else to tell Matt, other than the fact that I really did want to make long-distance work. I didn't know how, but I wasn't going to let that stop me. The universe would not have put Matthew John Elwes in my path to just yank him right back out again. I wouldn't fucking let it. We had seen off years of bullshit and finally admitted we had feelings for each other, and we had acted on them. This was only the beginning of this chapter, not the end.

I watched the pain on his face as his editor called a few times more over the course of the day. I talked to him about how this would all work out as he packed his stuff. I had never wanted to call Jess more and talk to her about what was happening and take her advice, but everything was moving so fast. By the late afternoon, Matt's car was packed, and he was ready to go.

We stood outside the farmhouse in the fading light, our arms around each other. I held him tight, hoping he realised I was going to find him being away from me just as hard as he was going to find being away from me. "I love you," I reminded him.

"I love you too." He smiled glumly.

Minutes passed, and neither of us said anything.

"So..." he started. "I guess I should get going."

"Yeah."

He got in, started the car, and wound the window down. "Do you think you could make it to London before I leave in a few days' time? Just to say a proper goodbye?"

I frowned at him and put my hand on his shoulder through the open car window. "I can, but it's not a goodbye, Matt. Not by a long shot."

He didn't agree or disagree, he just nodded. "Thank you."

Our gaze lingered for just a minute more before Matt looked away, and I knew it was time to go. I watched silently as his car drove out onto the lane, and down towards the road. I waved, and in the fading light, I saw his hand outstretched through the window of the car.

The second he was out of sight, I grabbed my phone from my pocket and called Jess.

'*So, you and he then?*'

"Yes, me and him, and it was worth it."

'*But he has to go on a business thing, a book tour, for three months?*'

"Minimum. More if he's doing well."

'*And you want him to do well?*'

"With everything I have."

'*Does he know how well you've done for yourself?*'

"That never really came up."

'*Too busy shagging, huh?*'

I chuckled. "Okay, I should have mentioned it."

'*Uh-huh.*' *She was judging me, and it was what I needed.*

'So, what are you going to do with this money you've made for yourself if you can't use it to help yourself?'

I didn't understand what she meant.

'Inheritance for Finn, I know, but what about you, Dean? When do you get to enjoy the fruits of all this work you've been putting into your business these last seven years?'

"What do you mean?" Jess had lost me.

'You have enough money in the bank, and a schedule with your son where you could easily get someone to cover the work you do for Emily. You could take yourself to Matt, for as long as Matt is away. That didn't cross your mind at all?'

It hadn't. "No." I thought about it for a moment. "But what about Finn?"

'He's here with me while you're working anyway. You come and spend time with him every chance you get around that schedule. Every weekend, every school holiday, every break you get. Why would being on a book tour with Matt be any different? You grab a load of cheap flights, and you run with it.'

I smirked. Was my ex actually telling me to spend money, go on a book tour with a new boyfriend, and live a little?

Jess knew my silences and understood how I thought just a little too well. 'And yes, I mean that you should have a damn life. You have been just you for long enough. This isn't just any fella off the street, Dean. This is Matt. This is the one you've wanted forever. Hire someone to do your glamping set up in Ullswater, and for the love of God, live your life for you. You only get one.'

It terrified me to admit it, but she was right. "You're such a smart arse genius. Remind me why we broke up?" I laughed.

'*Probably because I have no cock.*' She snorted.

"You're a crass asshole."

'*Mmmm,*' she agreed, '*but I'm also right!*'

She was, and I needed to make some plans. "Thank you. This is perfect."

I hung up the phone, thought about the logistics of it all. Jess was right. I had a lot of money in the bank from backing Emily in her business. It wasn't doing anything, and I hadn't done anything for myself in a very long time.

I'd have to find someone to take over for me here, and I would need to talk to Emily and let her know what I was going to do. This was going to be one hell of a plan. One I was determined to surprise Matt with the second I could.

Chapter Twenty-Seven
Matt

One Month Later

I sat in my hotel room in Paris and felt like the loneliest person on the planet. There I was in the romance capital of the world alone. Dean and I had been doing our best with the whole long-distance thing, but lately, I had been feeling a little out of place and like there was something he wasn't telling me. I knew he had been working a lot lately, and my insecurities just kept poking at me.

I grabbed my phone and texted him.

I wish you were here. I could really do with a hug xx

A few minutes later, my phone lit up with a reply.

I wish I was there too. I'd love to be hugging you, and a little more besides ;-)

I smirked at the reply. I would have done anything to have him there with me. I missed him terribly. The door of my room vibrated with a strong knock on it, and I assumed it must be the PR girl coming to harass me about some other detail since she was here to keep me on the straight and narrow as I toured Europe promoting my book.

Dark eyes, dark hair, and a beard greeted me with a grin when I pulled the door open with a sigh. It took a moment for my travel-weary brain to recognise him. The second it did, I pulled him tight against me, and I gasped, "What the hell are you doing here?"

"You said you needed a hug, so here I am." He smirked.

Damn, that was sexy. But I shook my head at him. "I'm so glad you're here."

"So am I," he breathed against my shoulder, leaning into me with his whole frame. "I've missed you, and I wanted to surprise you."

I pulled him through the open doorway and closed it. "Well, you have. And I've never been happier to be surprised in my life. I thought you were working."

He grinned. "I was, but I have someone covering for me. It's all good."

I hugged him tight again and let my body relax into his. I had really missed this man, and I wasn't ashamed to admit I almost cried in joy at having him in front of me.

"How long are you here for?" I needed to prepare myself for when he was leaving.

"Well, how long do you want me here for?"

"Can I keep you?" I laughed. It was a throwaway comment. I had missed him, and moving from place to place with just hired help wasn't as much fun as people would think.

"You can." He grinned.

At first, I didn't pick up on what he meant.

"I said, you can keep me," he repeated.

I still wasn't sure what he was getting at. My frown made that clear to him, and he walked towards the sofa to sit and explain.

"I've been arranging this since the moment you left the farmhouse. It just took a little longer than I was hoping it would. I've hired someone to do my work for me. I have flights booked to get back to Finn as often as I can and cleared it that you come with me for a lot of it. I'm here for as long as you want me."

This can't be real.

"Oh, is that right? And if I want you until the end of my book tour? Which they just announced this morning is going to take another three months." I huffed in disbelief.

"Then I guess I'm here for three months, or however long they want you."

No. I had to be hearing this wrong. "What about Emily's business? What about Finn?"

"Finn is always with his mum for school during the week anyway. I see him on school holidays and weekends and any time off I have. I can do it from all over the UK. I can do it from Europe. They have budget airlines, after all."

I stared at him.

"And as for Emily, *our* business will be just fine. I'm her silent partner. We made a tidy bit of money, and I've never done anything with mine until now. I've hired a guy. I've spent the last few weeks getting him up to speed. And here I am."

I leaned forward, put my hand on his shoulder, and nipped him as hard as I could.

"Owww!" He yelped with a laugh, pulling away from me. "You're not dreaming you, dickhead. I am real. This is happening."

I shrugged with a small smirk. "Just thought I would check."

"Uh-huh." He smirked, moving towards me again in a more predatory fashion.

"Always best to check." I breathed out as he got closer.

"Is that so?" His hands slid around my waist like they belonged there. "Maybe this will convince you." He crushed his mouth to mine and kissed me fiercely. I drank him in and responded in every way I could. He was here, he was staying, and I had missed him so damn much.

Epilogue
Dean

A year later

I SHIFTED NERVOUSLY on my feet as I glanced over at Jess, who was smirking.

"Fuck off," I whispered under my breath.

She grinned more. "Now, now. That's no way to talk to your best man."

I rolled my eyes. I knew I should have asked my cousin instead. I glanced over my shoulder and saw that everyone had arrived and was ready to begin.

Finn was first. He was carrying a pillow with our engraved wedding rings tied to them.

Toni and Emily were next, our bridesmaids.

Lastly, Matt was there with his dad and mum on either arm, his light grey suit matching mine. He was grinning, and I honestly didn't think I'd ever seen him happier.

When he arrived by my side, it was my turn to beam with pride. This was finally happening. I was getting married. We had talked about it. Matt was taking my name after the wedding. Everything was just amazing.

The celebrant stepped forward.

"Good morning. On behalf of Matthew Elwes and Dean Law, I would like to extend a warm welcome to you all gathered here to share in this wonderful day.

"My name is Ann-Marie, and I have the greatest honour of joining together the lives of these two men before us in matrimony."

Matt

Dean's hand shook as he slid the wedding band onto my finger. He told me he'd loved me for a long time, and how he wanted to be the man to share my life with for even longer still. My mum was in tears, and I had to admit that my own eyes were a little moist too.

My voice shook when I slid Dean's ring onto his finger. I told him I was proud of the man he was today, and I was honoured to have him at my side for all our tomorrows.

Ann-Marie smiled at us. "Matt and Dean, you have now both made a solemn and binding promise to one another in the presence of your witnesses, guests, and the registrar of marriages.

"It therefore gives me great pleasure to pronounce you are now husband and husband. Congratulations! You may now kiss each other!"

Dean leaned in and gave me a soft, sensual, yet chaste kiss on the lips. Finn, Jess, Emily, and Toni cheered and pulled on the strings of the party poppers they had with them. Paper streamers covered us, and everyone else in the room stood and clapped and cheered.

It had been a long time in the making, but as I walked back down the aisle hand in hand with my new husband, I realised I really was getting my very own happy ever after.

Other Books by Drew Duncan

Just Because Series

Because I Need You

Because I Want Him

Because I Didn't Know

Because It's Always You (Coming Soon)

Standalones

Hart Beats

EROTIC SHORTS

His Rules Series

Playing by the Rules

Changing the Rules

About the Author

Drew is an Irish author with a panache for sarcasm and a love of the random, her cynicism knows no bounds, but she's a secret hopeless romantic who likes to let her characters sizzle on the pages.

She lives her with two children, and dreams of escaping to Hampshire, the home of Jane Austen. When she's not writing, you can find her knitting, crocheting, shouting at Ireland playing rugby, and of course reading.

Keep up to date with all the latest releases and info from Drew by joining their mailing list here:
www.drewduncanbooks.co.uk/newsetter